MY BROTHER'S ENEMY

Firsts & Forever Stories Vol. 8

ALEXA LAND

Contents

Dedication

This is my 40th published book, and I'm dedicating it to my readers. Whether you've been reading my books for the last ten years, just discovered them, or something in between, thank you. I couldn't do this without you, and I'm so grateful you chose to give my stories a chance.

Acknowledgments

Thank you Kim, Melisha, Kelly, and Valerie for your help in making this book the best it can be. I truly appreciate your time and effort!

And thank you Amy for keeping me company along the way.

1

Romy

"Take a chance, Romy."

"Yeah, I don't think so."

"But that guy at the end of the bar keeps looking over here," my friend Pete said. "He's definitely interested, so you should go introduce yourself."

"Actually, he's been checking you out, not me."

No surprise there. Pete looked like a model with his bleached white-blond hair, big brown eyes, and high cheekbones. It didn't hurt that he was dressed in a tight, royal-blue T-shirt and shorts, which showed off his long, lean body. Meanwhile, I looked like a duck hanging out with a peacock—drab by comparison, especially in my baggy jeans and oversized sweatshirt.

He reached across the bar and refilled my coffee cup as he insisted, "You're wrong about that."

I snuck a glance at the guy in question, who was cute and probably in his mid-twenties. Ever since Pete had started working at my mom's bar, he'd been attracting a younger and hipper clientele. It was interesting to see them mingling with the regulars, including a number of senior citizens who'd been coming here for decades.

A minute later, the guy came over and slipped Pete his number.

Then he winked at him before heading for the door. Once he was gone, I said, "See?"

My friend looked disappointed as he muttered, "Oh," and swept the scrap of paper off the bar. But then he perked up again and asked, "What about that guy in the hockey jersey? I saw you checking him out when he came in."

"I was looking at the logo on his chest, and wondering which team had a super pissed off saber-toothed tiger as its mascot."

"The Nashville Predators."

"You just made that up."

"Nope. It's a real team."

"And you know that why?"

"Because I watch hockey." He raised a brow and asked, "Why do you look surprised?"

"I just remember how much you hated all things sports-related when we were in high school."

"I've broadened my horizons in the nearly ten years since we graduated. In this case, I started watching hockey while dating a guy who was totally into it. I ended up kicking him to the curb after a month or two, but my love of hockey lives on."

Pete and I had been friends in our teens, but we'd drifted apart after high school and gotten back in touch just a couple of months ago. He really had changed a lot over the years, while I was pretty sure I was exactly the same.

He went back to scanning the crowd. Then he indicated a tall guy by the restrooms and asked, "What about him? He's cute. You should go over and introduce yourself."

"Once again, I'll pass."

"Why?"

"We've talked about this, Pete. I'm not interested in meeting anyone."

He shook his head. "I know what you said, but come on. So, you've had a string of bad relationships. Who hasn't? That doesn't mean you should give up on love, not at twenty-seven. It's bad enough that you never go out, and—"

"I'm out right now!"

"This doesn't count. It would if you got your flirt on while you were here, but you only come in to visit me or your mom. And then the rest of the time, you're either at work or home alone in your depressing apartment."

"How is my apartment depressing?"

Pete shrugged. "It's small, and you live alone."

I was about to argue that it was small *because* I lived alone, and how much space did one person need? But one of the bar's regulars joined us just then, greeting me with a back-slapping embrace as he exclaimed, "Romy, my boy! Good to see you!" The little old man let go of me and grabbed Pete's hand, shaking it vigorously as he said, "I'm Henry Kissinger—not the famous one." He'd been introducing himself that way all my life. Probably longer.

"Pete DiChanza. What can I make you, Mr. Kissinger?"

"Hot tea with brandy. Mandy knows how I like it, but I guess she isn't in today."

"No sir, my boss went out to dinner with her fiancé," Pete said. "But if you walk me through it, I'll remember your drink order for next time."

After Henry explained his usual—black tea with two sugars and a splash of apple brandy—he turned to me and said, "I've been with my sister in Arizona. She fell and broke her hip. Terrible, at our age."

"I'm so sorry."

"She's fine now," he said, "so I came back home, and everything's different here at the bar! Don't get me wrong, I'm happy your mom got engaged and has been taking some time off. I always told her she worked too much. But I feel like I missed a lot in the few months I was gone, including some big excitement. A couple of the fellas were just filling me in." He gestured at a pair of regulars in their seventies, who could be found in their favorite booth most evenings. "They said back in October, two hoodlums with baseball bats came in and started smashing up the bar. They also said it was meant to be a message to your brother, Adriano."

"Yeah, but don't worry," I said. "The criminal behind the attack hasn't been heard from in almost three months, and I really don't think he'll cause any more trouble."

"Oh, I'm not worried," Henry said. "I'm just sorry I wasn't here to defend your mom and the bar when it all went down." He was so frail that a light breeze could probably knock him over, but it was a sweet sentiment.

"Fortunately, they didn't go after Mandy or any of her patrons," Pete said. "They just smashed up some furniture and the bottles behind the bar. Someone called 911 right away, and the thugs ran off as soon as they heard the sirens."

"But my buddies told me the man behind the attack was never arrested," Henry said. "What's to stop him from doing it again?"

Pete's dark eyes sparkled with excitement. If there was one thing my friend loved, it was the opportunity to gossip. "He wouldn't dare. I'll explain why, but let me back up a minute. Around the same time this lowlife, Mario Greco, sent his men to smash up the bar, he also had them kidnap Adriano. I don't know if you heard that part."

Henry's watery eyes went wide, and he exclaimed, "No! Is he okay?"

Pete nodded. "He's fine. He ended up escaping, but that gives you an idea of the type of criminal we're talking about here."

Henry was hanging on every word. "Then what happened?"

Pete's flair for the dramatic was becoming more apparent by the moment. "Eventually, Adriano managed to track this guy down by getting help from the Dombruso family, his long-lost relatives on his late father's side. I guess they're bigtime gangsters or something. Anyway, there was a high-speed car chase, followed by a confrontation between Adriano and Greco. I saw the whole thing. Adriano told this guy he'd kill him if he ever showed his face again, and the Dombrusos were there to back him up. That must have put the fear of god into him, because Greco hasn't been seen since."

"That's not exactly what my brother said," I pointed out. "I wasn't there, but I heard about it from Adriano. He basically just told this guy to leave town, or he'd be sorry."

"Well, yes," Pete conceded, as he made a cup of tea, "but killing him was implied in the 'he'd be sorry' part."

4

I shook my head. "My brother might break the law from time to time, but he's not a murderer."

"Of course not," he said, "but I'm pretty sure his mafia relatives could make that guy disappear with a single phone call. I think Greco knew it too, and that's why he backed off."

Henry turned to me and asked, "Is that true? Are they really in the mafia?"

"I'm not sure." The old man looked skeptical, so I added, "Adriano only recently met them, and since he and I had different dads, I don't have much to do with his father's relatives. Plus, I wasn't directly involved in most of this, so I don't have a lot of details. You know how overprotective Adriano is. He didn't want me to get hurt, so he made a point of keeping me out of the loop when all of this was going down."

The old man grinned at that. "Yeah, he really is protective of you. I remember when you were a kid and some bully in the neighborhood was giving you a hard time. Your big brother scared him so bad that the kid wet his pants and ran home crying."

I almost asked which time he was referring to, because stuff like that had happened a lot. I'd been small for my age and an easy target for bullies, while Adriano was huge and ten years older than me.

Pete placed the mug of tea on the bar, added a very generous splash of brandy, and said, "Here you go, Mr. Kissinger. It's on the house. Let me know how I did, so I can be sure to get it right next time."

Henry looked delighted as he picked up the cup and said, "I can already tell it's perfect, kid. Do it just like that next time. Oh, and welcome. I can tell you're going to be a great addition to this place."

As Henry returned to the booth where his friends were waiting, I asked Pete, "Could you please tone down that story a bit, the next time you tell it? You made my brother sound like Al Capone."

"Okay, but he really is a bit of a gangster. The old-timers in this neighborhood have known both you and your brother all your lives, so I'm sure they've noticed."

Maybe he had a point. Until recently, Adriano had run an illegal gambling operation, and he'd definitely cultivated a tough guy persona to go with it. That business was what had put him in an actual gangster's crosshairs. But when Mario Greco had tried to pull off a hostile takeover, he'd found more than he'd bargained for in Adriano Dombruso.

I checked the time on my phone, finished my coffee, and tucked a five-dollar bill under the mug. "I'd better go," I said. "I'm working the late shift tonight."

"Take your money back. You know your mom's rule—family drinks for free."

"It's for you. Thanks for all the refills."

"You don't have to do that, either."

"I want to. See you soon, Pete."

As I cut through the bar, he called, "We need to go to a club next weekend and find you a man! I'll loan you an outfit. I suspect there's a hot bod under those huge sweatshirts you always wear."

The regulars thought that was pretty funny. It wasn't news to any of them that I was gay. It definitely wasn't news that I was single, either.

Right before I reached the exit, an old-timer named Lester asked me, "Why don't you date Pete? He's a nice kid, and what my niece would call a real fox." I'd met his niece. She was in her fifties, and I could easily imagine her saying that.

How could I answer this without explaining we were both bottoms, and if I was going to date anyone, it'd be a big, burly top? I left it at, "We're too much alike, Les," and stepped through the door.

I'd parked in the street since the narrow lot was pretty full, and after I reached my truck I paused for a moment and looked around. This working class neighborhood was probably the last thing most people would picture when they thought of Las Vegas. Instead of glitzy casinos and bright lights, all I saw in either direction were small houses, aging apartment buildings, and a few mom and pop businesses struggling to stay afloat.

I'd been here all my life—literally right here. My first twenty-two years were spent in the apartment above the bar, and after I graduated from UNLV I moved into an apartment that was barely five minutes away. No wonder I felt restless. This wasn't the time to dwell on that though, so I tried to push it aside as I slid behind the wheel.

It was just past sunset on a Saturday night, and even in the off-season, traffic around the Strip would be annoying. I swung wide to avoid that entire area as I drove to the opposite end of town.

The ambulance company I worked for had opened their newest location just a couple of months ago. The state-of-the-art building was in an upscale neighborhood, one I'd had very little reason to visit before being transferred here.

All three ambulance bays were empty when I went inside. That meant all the crews currently on duty were out on calls—a sure sign it was going to be a busy night.

I poured myself what had to be my eighth coffee of the day before heading to the locker room. Then I changed into my dark blue uniform and matching windbreaker before checking my reflection in the mirror on the wall.

What I saw made me frown. I usually wore my light brown hair really short, but it was at least a month past needing a cut. Also, the fact that I hadn't been sleeping enough was written all over me, from my pale skin to the shadows under my hazel eyes. So much for the New Year's resolution I'd made just three weeks ago to take better care of myself.

When someone entered the locker room, I turned away from the mirror. A moment later, my partner Julio came around the corner and exclaimed, "Therefore art thou, Romeo!" He found endless amusement in my name.

I grinned at him and asked, "So, when your son was born, did the terrible dad jokes kick in automatically? Or did they develop gradually over time?"

"Come on, that was funny! Admit it," he said, as he opened his locker.

"Maybe the first five times you said it."

"No way have I said that five times."

"You're right. It's more like ten."

"Okay, but that's only twice a year, given how long we've been partners."

"True." I picked up my coffee cup and took a sip before asking, "Why are you here so early?"

"My kid was practicing the drums we got him for Christmas, so I had to run for my life. What's your excuse?"

"I was visiting a friend who's working at my mom's bar, and he kept talking about finding me a man. I needed to bail out of that conversation, so I left and came here."

"That reminds me. My barber's cousin is gay, and we were going to slip him your number. He says——"

I cut him off with, "Why is everyone so interested in my love life? There's nothing wrong with being single."

Julio knit his thick, dark brows. "I'd agree if you seemed happy, but honestly dude? You really don't."

"I appreciate the concern, but I'm fine."

It didn't seem like he believed me, but he let it drop and finished changing into his uniform. Then we chatted in the lounge for a while, until it was time to clock in and go to work.

The start of our shift was perfectly routine. I had no way of knowing that what would happen next would change my life forever.

2

Marcus

My flight from New York to Las Vegas got in just before midnight. From there, it was a short cab ride to the Bellagio—my home until I figured out what was next for me.

I was way too restless to sleep and ended up pacing in my suite, until it started to feel like the walls were closing in. Since my cars were in storage, I placed a call to the concierge, who produced a rented convertible within the hour. That was one of my favorite things about Vegas—I could get whatever I wanted, even in the middle of the night.

After picking a direction at random, I started driving. In a matter of minutes, the city lights were in my rearview mirror, and the desert was all around me.

The Porsche's speedometer slid past ninety, then a hundred. The engine revved, and the wind whipped my hair and raised goose-bumps up and down my arms. I welcomed the cold, because it woke me up and made me feel alive.

Even though returning to Vegas had probably been a mistake, I'd missed this while I was in New York. That city felt claustro-phobic to me, but I could breathe out here, under the wide-open sky. There'd been a time in my life when I could only dream about this kind of freedom. Now, it was impossible to take it for granted.

I might have driven until dawn. Hell, I might have driven forever, if it wasn't for a scrawny coyote that wandered onto the highway. My breath caught when he appeared in my headlights, and I yanked the wheel to the right as I slammed on the brakes. The Porsche bounced hard as it left the pavement, and then it skidded across the dirt in a wide arc. Fortunately, there was nothing to run into, apart from a few scraggly bushes that snapped beneath my tires.

By the time the car came to a stop, I'd spun around so far that I was at a ninety-degree angle to the highway. The coyote was in my headlights again, and he looked back at me curiously before trotting off in the opposite direction.

I let out the breath I'd been holding and muttered, "Fucking hell."

Once my pulse settled back down, I pulled back onto the blacktop and returned to the city at a more reasonable speed. Apparently I wasn't quite done being reckless though, because when I was back inside the city limits and realized what part of town I was in, I took a left turn and drove someplace I really should have avoided.

The reason I'd left Vegas a couple of months ago was because I'd had a run-in with a two-bit criminal. He was the head of an illegal gambling operation, and I'd made a move on his territory, thinking it'd be easy pickings.

Little did I know he was actually the illegitimate son of a big-time mobster, which made him part of one of the most powerful crime families on the west coast. When I pushed, he pushed back harder, with a whole team of his gangster relatives as back-up. The only thing to do after that was to clear out and let the dust settle.

I probably should have stayed gone, because this shit wasn't worth getting killed over. And I definitely shouldn't be taking this detour past his family's bar, to see if he happened to be there after hours. That was all kinds of stupid.

But because I had a little fantasy of catching this guy alone and punching him in the face, I kept going until I reached the bar. Even though it was nearly three a.m., there was a light on and someone was inside, so I pulled to the curb.

It wasn't the douchebag criminal, though. Instead, it was a guy dressed in a dark blue jacket that was too big on him. I watched as he retrieved a bottle, then took a seat at the bar. He sat facing away from the door and the plate glass window, so it was easy to read the three big letters on the back of his windbreaker—EMT.

When my former crew had done some research into my enemy —badly, since they'd failed to discover his mafia connection—they'd told me he had a younger brother who worked as a medic. That had to be him.

Since we'd never met, I could probably get away with talking to him. I'd heard the illegal gambling operation had closed up shop, but I wanted to confirm it. Any other information I could gain would be a bonus.

I climbed out of the car and approached the simple, two-story building, watching to make sure this guy really was alone. The last thing I needed was big brother barging in on our conversation and catching me with my guard down.

When I reached the door, I realized this guy had left his keys in the lock. That was perfect, because now I had an excuse to strike up a conversation. I removed them before stepping inside.

The bar's sole occupant was slumped on his stool and didn't hear me enter. There was an empty whiskey bottle beside him, which suggested he'd been at this a while. He poured a shot from the new bottle he'd just helped himself to and tossed it back. Then he crossed his arms on the bar top and rested his head on them.

I hadn't planned to sneak up on him. But as I crossed the bar, I was so focused on listening to make sure no one else was in the building that I didn't let him know I was there. No wonder he seemed startled when he turned around and discovered me just a few feet away.

And as soon as I got a good look at him, I probably seemed as startled as he did. He was beautiful. More than that. Ethereal, that was the word for it—as delicate and unexpected as an angel on earth.

As I drew closer, I saw that his wide-set eyes were green and gold and brown, like a perfect fall day. They were also brimming with tears. There was so much raw emotion in them that it was jarring. It was a little like seeing someone stark naked out on the street—he seemed so vulnerable that my first impulse was to wrap him in a blanket and try to protect him.

We both just stared at each other for a few seconds, until he mumbled, "We…um, we're closed."

"No, I know," I stammered. That was all I could think to say for a moment, as I tried to swim up from the depths of pain and despair in his eyes. Then I remembered the item clutched in my hand and held it out to him. "Your keys were in the door."

"Oh. Thank you."

He made no move to take them, so I placed them on the bar. After another pause, I asked, "Are you alright?"

He shook his head and tried to reach for the bottle of whiskey, but he knocked it over. As it began to spill, I lunged forward and righted it. We were very close together now, and he looked up at me as the tears overflowed and tumbled down his cheeks.

It was like a dam broke. He began sobbing so hard that his entire body shook. At the same time, he tipped forward, burying his face in my chest as he clutched my dark suit jacket with both hands.

At first, I didn't know what to do. I really wasn't equipped for stuff like this. I held my hands up, as if someone was pointing a gun at me, while he kept sobbing.

Okay, clearly I had to do something to try to comfort him. When I awkwardly put an arm around his shoulders, he grabbed me in a hug and began sobbing even harder. The way he clung to me made my heart ache, in a way I couldn't really explain.

For lack of any better ideas, I tried stroking his hair, which turned out to be really soft. Surprisingly, that actually seemed to soothe him. His sobs tapered off, and I let myself relax a bit.

After a while, I told him, "If someone hurt you, I can go beat the shit out of them for you." Seriously. I was good at that, and terrible at whatever I should be doing in this moment.

But he shook his head and mumbled, "My dad died."

"I'm sorry. Were you close?" It possibly wasn't the right question to ask in this situation, but it was out of my mouth before I realized that.

"No. I never met him before tonight."

"I don't understand."

"I was at work. I'm an EMT," he said, by way of explanation.

"Yeah, I figured that out."

"How?"

"The uniform was a tip-off, especially the big, neon yellow letters on your back."

He let go of me and sat up a bit. Then he looked down at himself and lifted the flap of his jacket. When he did that, I glimpsed a plastic name tag which said "R. Russo," above a patch with the name of a local ambulance service.

"I was supposed to change before I left work." He began patting his pockets as he muttered, "I hope I didn't forget my stuff."

"What stuff?"

"My phone and wallet. They were in my locker." He got up and immediately tripped over something, hitting the floor with an, "Ow." I moved his stool aside as he shifted around and leaned against the bar. Then he put an open duffle bag on his lap, pulled a phone out of it, and announced, "Found it."

"That's good. Want me to help you up?"

"No. I like it down here," he said, as he set aside the bag and phone. "The room isn't spinning as much from this angle."

"Did you drink all this whiskey? If so, I should maybe take you to the hospital," I said, as I held up the empty bottle.

He squinted at it as he knit his brows. Then he shook his head and told me, "It was half-empty when I started. I only had, like, five shots. Maybe six. Possibly seven…"

I crouched down and studied him closely. "I hope it wasn't seven. That's way too much for someone your size."

He turned his head to look at me, and it was like he was seeing me for the first time. "I don't know you." I shook my head, and he asked, "What's your name?"

"Marcus. What's yours?" I'd known I wasn't going to go with my most frequently used alias, but I surprised myself by giving him my real name. Not that it mattered, since it seemed unlikely he'd remember any of this in the morning.

"Romy."

"Is that short for something?"

"Romeo, but nobody calls me that, thank god. I don't even know why my mom chose it. It's not like she's into Shakespeare or anything."

"Did you ask her?"

He nodded. "She said she liked the way it sounded with our last name, but there has to be more to it than that, don't you think? A name is supposed to mean something."

"Is it?"

"I think so. Does your name have a meaning?"

"I doubt it."

He considered that before asking, "Do people call you Marc?"

"No. Never."

"Okay, then I won't either. It's too plain for you anyway. You don't look like a Marc, but you do look like a Marcus. It's a noble name. Makes me think of Marcus Aurelius. That suits you for sure."

I grinned a little and asked, "The name of a Roman emperor suits me?"

He nodded, and then he shifted around so he was on his knees, facing me. When he started to reach for me, I flinched. I couldn't help it. Then he said softly, "It's okay, Marcus. I won't hurt you."

That should have been funny. I was a huge guy, and he was this fragile little thing. How could he possibly hurt me? Somehow though, it came across as very sweet.

He proceeded to brush my hair out of my eyes before tracing one of my sideburns and lightly skimming my jaw. "Definitely noble," he murmured, still on his random tangent. Then he asked, "Are you Latino?"

"In part. I'm also Greek and Italian, according to one of those who-the-fuck-am-I genetic screenings, but then my last name is English or Irish. Between all of that, I guess I'm basically a mutt."

"You're beautiful, Marcus," he murmured, as his finger outlined my lower lip. "I'd be afraid to talk to you if I wasn't really drunk. Gorgeous men always intimidate me." Romy pulled back his hand and looked embarrassed. "I should stop, because I'm probably making this weird. You're not supposed to randomly touch strangers, and you're definitely not supposed to cry on them. I know this, even if my inhibitions seem to have clocked out."

He sat back down on the floor and leaned against the bar, and I sat beside him and said, "It's okay. You're obviously having a rough night."

"Horrible."

"Want to talk about it?"

He glanced at me and asked, "Do you really want to hear this?"

"Sure."

Romy looked away again and began fidgeting with the hem of his windbreaker. "I went out on what should have been a routine call tonight, a heart attack. We got there too late, though. I performed CPR but the man died, right there on his living room rug with his wife crying her eyes out beside him.

"His name was Dave Johnson, which normally wouldn't even register with me because it's such a common name. But then his wife called him Hitch. I'd heard that nickname before, so I looked around the room and there was this couple's wedding portrait on the mantel. It was maybe twenty-five years old, judging by the clothes and hairstyles, and that was when I realized who he was. He'd aged badly. I would have walked right by him on the street without recognizing him. But in that wedding picture, he looked exactly like the man in the photo my mom had saved for me."

"Of your father?"

Romy nodded. "He bailed when she got pregnant—told her he was moving to Philly to go to work for his uncle, and that was the last she heard from him. Except, it turns out he just moved across

15

town. Not long after, he married someone else, had two more kids, and forgot all about me. I pieced the story together, between the things his wife was saying and the rest of the photos on the mantel. Not that I told her any of this, of course. She had enough to deal with."

I muttered, "He was an asshole," and Romy glanced at me again.

"I know, and just to be clear, I didn't need him or want anything from him. My mom and brother took good care of me when I was growing up. But would it have been so hard to come and see me? Just once. He knew where to find me. This bar's been here almost forty years, and my mom's name is right above the door. It's literally called Mandy's Place." Romy sighed, and after a pause he added, "I tried searching for him a few times over the years, but it was impossible to find him. His name was just too common, and I didn't have a way of narrowing it down."

"Maybe it's for the best. That deadbeat didn't deserve you."

"You're right, he didn't, and I was better off without him. But then, why does this hurt so much?"

He started crying again, silently this time. Somehow, that was worse than the sobbing. When I put my arm around his shoulders, he curled into me. It didn't feel awkward this time.

We stayed like that for a while, before I suggested, "You might feel better after you get some rest."

He nodded and mumbled, "I'm exhausted." Then he sat up and met my gaze with anguish in his eyes. "Will you please stay with me? I don't want to be alone tonight."

How could I possibly say no to that? I had to ask, though. "Are you really willing to bring a stranger into your home?" Not that I'd ever hurt him, not in a million years. But I wanted to know he generally made better decisions than this.

He shrugged. "All my single friends invite strangers over all the time—people they meet on dating apps. How is this different?"

As I got to my feet and helped him up, I said, "That's a terrible idea too, and I hope you don't do that."

"I don't."

It turned out he was taller than I'd expected—about five-eleven or so, but I had a good four inches and at least sixty pounds on him. He swayed unsteadily, and I caught him and asked, "Where are we going?"

"Really? You're staying?" When I nodded, he said, "Upstairs, to my mom's apartment."

"Are we going to wake anyone if we go up there?" His homicidal brother, for example.

"No. The apartment's been empty for a couple of months, ever since Mom moved in with her fiancé."

Romy went to reach for his duffle bag and almost fell over. I picked it up for him and hung it on my shoulder, and then I steadied him with an arm around his waist. He grabbed his keys and somehow remembered to lock the front door before saying, "Okay, here we go."

We cut through the kitchen, and at the back of the building, a narrow staircase led to a small landing. He dropped his keys twice, so I unlocked the door to the apartment for him.

As I followed him inside, he said, "Just so you know, I don't live here anymore. If my room seems childish, it's because I hung on to some stuff from when I was little." I didn't know why my opinion would matter to him one way or another.

His small bedroom was cozy, with light blue walls, shelves crowded with books, and mismatched furniture. The only thing that made it seem like a kid's room was the well-worn teddy bear on the twin bed.

As I put his bag on the desk, he muttered, "I really need a shower. I always take one right after work."

"Is that the best idea? What if you fall over or pass out?"

He considered that as he pulled some clothes out of the dresser. Then he told me, "I'll probably be okay, but I'll leave the bathroom door open just in case. If you hear a crash, please come check on me."

That wasn't reassuring, and I paced and listened closely while he was in the shower across the hall. Fortunately, he didn't take long. Less than ten minutes later, he reappeared wearing a UNLV T-shirt that was way too big on him, along with a pair of gym shorts that had seen better days.

He climbed into the narrow bed and wrapped his arms around the teddy bear. His lids started to get heavy right away as he mumbled, "Promise me you'll be here when I wake up."

There were many excellent reasons to say no to that. What if his brother came by in the morning? I was cornered and unarmed, and he'd probably try to kill me if he found me here. Or what if Romy ended up blacking out and forgetting we'd met? He certainly seemed drunk enough to do that. Wouldn't he freak out when he woke up and found a stranger in his room?

Somehow though, I couldn't stand the thought of him waking up to an empty apartment, not when he seemed so vulnerable. I tried asking, "Isn't there anyone you could call to come over and stay with you? A friend or relative, maybe?"

He shook his head. "I want it to be you."

"Why?"

"Because you make me feel safe."

Fucking hell, this guy had terrible instincts. Who in their right mind, drunk or not, would take one look at me and come to that conclusion? It was like deciding a wolf would make a good house pet.

He whispered, "Please, Marcus."

Fine. He had me, and damn the consequences. I pulled the desk chair over to his bedside, sat down, and told him, "I'll be right here when you wake up. I promise."

A look of relief crossed his beautiful face, and he whispered, "Thank you," before shutting his eyes. He shifted a little, settling in with that raggedy teddy bear, and fell asleep moments later.

I pulled up his blanket a little higher, so it covered his shoulder. Then I sat back and sighed.

What a strange, confusing evening. I really shouldn't be here... except that something about this man called to me, and I felt compelled to answer. It was a weird mix of attraction and an overwhelming need to protect and take care of him, which was totally unfamiliar to me.

But whether or not I understood it, that need kept me right there at his bedside, watching over Romy while he slept. This definitely wasn't one of my better ideas. But maybe it would be okay, as long as he never found out I was the man his brother knew as Mario Greco.

3

Romy

It was no surprise that I woke up with a pounding headache, given how much I'd had to drink the night before. What *was* a surprise? The gorgeous man asleep at my bedside.

In a moment of weakness, I'd begged him to stay, and for some reason he'd actually done it. He must be so uncomfortable too, given the way he was awkwardly folded into my wooden chair. I had no idea how he'd even managed to doze off like that.

Embarrassment washed over me as I set aside my teddy bear. Clearly, I'd made no effort to hide the fact that I was a dork. Then I sat up and studied my visitor. He was probably in his early thirties, with a slightly olive complexion and jet black hair that was long enough to graze his collar. His sideburns were also on the long side and seemed a bit retro, but they suited him somehow. Honestly, a man that good-looking could do just about anything and still be absolutely striking.

He'd taken off his suit jacket and used it as a blanket, and when he shifted it started to slide off of him. Reflexively, I lunged forward and tried to grab it. Some combination of those things woke him and he leapt up, knocking over the chair in the process. He staggered backwards until he ran into my bookshelves, and then he looked around with his fists raised and fear in his eyes.

Good thing I knew how to deal with people who were panicked and disoriented. It was something I encountered pretty frequently on the job, and I'd been trained for it.

"We met last night, Marcus. My name is Romy Russo," I told him, as I took a seat on the edge of the bed and held my hands where he could see them. "You're in my mom's apartment, which is above her bar."

He focused on me and repeated, in a rough whisper, "Romy."

I nodded and picked up his suit jacket. Then I stood up slowly and held it out to him. "I'm going to use the bathroom, and after that I'm going to go see if there's anything to eat. Join me in the kitchen whenever you're ready." He took the jacket from me, and I looked up at him and smiled before leaving the room.

By the time he appeared in the kitchen doorway, I'd brewed a pot of tea and searched all the cupboards looking for anything that might pass as breakfast. He'd put on his jacket and combed his hair, and his expression could best be described as sheepish. "Sorry about earlier," he said. "I was pretty disoriented when I woke up."

"I'm sure it didn't help that I was lunging at you just as you opened your eyes. For the record, your jacket slipped off and I was trying to catch it."

"It's funny," he said, as his gaze slid around the vintage yellow and white kitchen. "I was worried you wouldn't remember last night, so I thought I'd be the one trying to calm you down this morning, after you woke up to find a stranger in your bedroom."

"No, I remember everything," I muttered. "I almost wish I didn't." I changed the subject by gesturing at the table. "The cupboards were pretty bare, but I made us some tea and off-brand Pop Tarts."

"Thanks, but maybe I should go. I'm sure you want to call your family if you haven't already, so you can tell them what happened."

"Actually, I'm not ready to talk to them about my dad. I'll call my mom after I take some time to process it, but not now."

"And your brother?"

"I'm definitely going to wait to tell him," I said, as I retrieved a bottle of ibuprofen from one of the cabinets. "We had different dads, so this doesn't directly affect him. But he's really overprotective of me, so if I call him and seem upset he'll probably rush back from San Francisco to make sure I'm okay. There's no need for that right now."

Marcus crossed the kitchen and took a seat at the table, and I joined him and poured the tea into a pair of mismatched mugs. Mine was decorated with a picture of one of the casinos—though we'd actually gotten it at a garage sale—and his was something the bar's liquor distributor had given us. I started to hand it to him, but then I muttered, "Oops, that one has a chip in it," and gave him the other one instead. Since he was wearing a suit that clearly cost thousands of dollars, I had to wonder what he thought of this funky apartment. He seemed pretty comfortable, though.

When I shook a couple of Advil into my hand, he glanced at me and asked, "How do you feel?"

"Not great, but I'll live."

"Do you have to work today?"

"No. Whenever we encounter something that's considered a traumatic incident while on the job, a whole protocol kicks in. The first step was meeting with my supervisor last night. He dragged himself out of bed at one a.m., after my partner called and told him what happened. I was given a mandatory week off, which is company policy, and I'll have to meet with a counselor before I'll be allowed to go back to work."

I washed the pills down with some tea before adding, "Obviously, dispatch would never knowingly send an EMT on a call involving a family member. But no one knew what I was walking into last night, including me."

"I see."

"Can I ask what you do? It seems I did most of the talking last night."

He paused for a moment before answering. "A few different things. Lately, I've been putting in a lot of time as the executor of my mentor's estate."

"I'm so sorry for your loss."

"It's been almost two years since he died. He left quite a few loose ends though, so it's taking some time."

"Can I ask what happened?"

"Cancer. He was seventy-four, and he knew the end was coming for months. It gave him time to tell me exactly what he wanted me to do after he passed."

"It's nice of you to put so much time into carrying out his instructions."

He broke eye contact, and after a pause, he said, "Actually, he was the closest thing to a father I had, and I owe him. He had my back when nobody else did. He also left me a fortune. I've been trying to honor his wishes, but…sometimes I don't know if I can do all he asked of me."

There was a lot of emotion behind those words, and I said, "I'm sure you're doing your best." That seemed trite and unhelpful, but I didn't know what else to say.

"I shouldn't even be talking about this. You're the one who just suffered a loss."

"But I appreciate you opening up to me."

"You're really easy to talk to," he muttered.

"So are you." After a pause, I said, "Since I have some unexpected time off, I think I'll drive to the coast and spend a couple of days in Southern California. I could use a change of scenery, and the thought of being by the ocean seems…I don't know. Soothing, I guess."

"That sounds like a great idea."

"Would you like to come with me?" I just had to ask. I'd never forgive myself if I let this gorgeous man walk right back out of my life. To try to convince him, I added, "It seems like you've been dealing with some pretty intense stuff, so maybe you could use a break, too."

He seemed surprised. "Wouldn't you want to ask a friend to go with you?"

"I just did. I know we just met, but I like you, Marcus, and I really want to get to know you. This would give us the perfect opportunity."

He held my gaze for a long moment. It was hard to tell what was going through his mind, but finally he said, "I'll come along on one condition."

"What's that?"

"You let me pay for everything."

"Can I ask why?"

"I just don't want to feel like I'm taking advantage of you."

"You wouldn't be. But if that's important to you, then sure."

"There's also something I need to say up front." Marcus seemed to choose his words carefully. "I can't promise you anything beyond these next few days, Romy."

"I know, and it's fine." That didn't surprise me. Neither of us knew where this was going to go, so he really didn't have to worry about leading me on.

After breakfast, we made plans for him to pick me up at my apartment in an hour, so we'd both have time to pack a bag. I walked him downstairs, and he said, "See you soon," before heading out the door.

As I watched him get in his car and drive away, an insecure little part of me wondered if I'd ever see him again. Maybe all of this had been painfully awkward for him, and maybe he'd instantly regretted agreeing to spend the next couple of days with me. After all, I was just some random guy he'd met a few hours ago, and I'd spent most of that time either drunk or asleep.

Asking him to go on a little road trip with me must have seemed like such an odd request. It had been impulsive and not at all like me, but I had to shoot my shot. Never mind that I'd claimed to have sworn off men and dating. When I'd made that pledge, I never imagined a man like Marcus might come into my life.

It wasn't just that he was handsome. He was kind, too. I was impressed by the way he'd listened to me, then sat at my bedside all night to make sure I was okay. He was something special, and I looked forward to spending time with him and getting to know him.

But first, I really needed him to show up.

4

Marcus

What the hell was I doing?

Had I really agreed to go away with the brother of my sworn enemy? And what would happen if Romy found out who I was?

Actually, there was no mystery there—he'd hate me for the things that had been done to his family in my name. Never mind that my crew had gone rogue and done things I never would have condoned, including smashing up his mother's bar and taking his brother hostage. That was still on me, and Romy wouldn't be interested in excuses about my men running amok while I was on the east coast.

Despite that—despite everything—I really wanted to spend some time with him. He was sweet, beautiful, and intriguing, and being with him felt good, so why not? After all, it was just a couple of days.

I'd been surprised when he asked me to go away with him, but that actually worked out perfectly. If we tried to spend time together in Vegas, I'd constantly have to look over my shoulder. Even though his brother was currently in San Francisco, Adriano Dombruso had confronted me a couple of months ago with at least two dozen relatives and hired guns in tow. I had no idea which of those people

25

were a regular part of Romy's life, but any of them could recognize me and spill my secret. Then Romy would despise me, and his gangster relatives would probably try to shoot me. Obviously, all of that was best avoided.

So, getting out of Vegas with him made sense. Besides, I could really use some down-time, and I didn't have many chances to step outside Mario Greco's high-pressure world. I'd spent the last two years trying to fulfill the promises I'd made to a dead man—who'd left me both a fortune and a mountain of responsibilities I couldn't ignore—and it was wearing me down.

But I really didn't want to think about that right now.

Instead, I returned to the Bellagio and focused on getting ready for my trip. I showered and shaved, then put on a black t-shirt and jeans, along with a vintage motorcycle jacket. I liked this version of myself, and I didn't get to see it very often. Lately, it had all been about business suits, meetings, and deals, and I was tired of playing that part.

Once I was dressed, I frowned at my reflection in the bathroom mirror. When I tried to fix my hair I made it worse, so I tried again. Now it was a real mess. After battling my hair for another minute or two, I made myself step away from the mirror and leave it alone.

I was nervous to the point of feeling slightly queasy, probably because all of this was so unfamiliar to me. I never dated…though I might possibly be wrong in thinking this was a date. Maybe Romy had just asked me to come along as a friend. And maybe I should really stop overthinking it.

After repacking my luggage and checking out of the hotel, I drove to his apartment. He was waiting outside for me, dressed in jeans and a dark blue hoodie that was so big, it would have fit me with room to spare.

A look of relief crossed his features when I pulled up and cut the engine. Had he expected me to be a no-show?

"This is such a nice car," he said, as he stuffed a backpack and his small duffle bag into the nearly nonexistent back seat.

"It's a rental. Want to drive?"

His eyes went wide. "Are you serious?"

I climbed out of the Porsche and held the door for him, and he was smiling as he slid behind the wheel. He then proceeded to obey every traffic law on our way out of town. Even once we were out on the open road, he stayed within ten miles of the speed limit.

"Go ahead and open it up if you want to," I said. "If you get a speeding ticket, I'll pay it."

"I shouldn't. It wouldn't be safe."

"There's nobody out here, and this is a flat stretch of highway. We'll be fine."

He considered that, then accelerated to eleven miles above the speed limit. It seemed to make him happy, so I didn't complain. Instead, I found a classic rock station on the radio, turned my face toward the sun, and let myself relax.

It was loud with the top down, between the roar of the engine and the wind, so we didn't talk much those first couple of hours. Eventually, we decided to stop for lunch and ended up at a colorful Mexican restaurant just off the highway. It featured a fountain in the entryway, painted tiles on nearly every surface, and orange vinyl booths. Plastic plants and fake stuffed parrots rounded out the décor.

We were the only customers and were given a large booth at the back of the dining room. Once we took a seat, Romy looked around like this was the most fascinating place he'd ever seen. Then he began reading the huge menu as he murmured, "I have no idea what to order. Everything sounds terrific, and it smells so good in here." After a while, he looked up at me and asked, "Would you maybe want to get the shrimp fajita feast for two?" Then he quickly added, "If not, that's totally fine."

When I said, "Great idea, let's do that," a gorgeous smile lit up his face. Then his phone buzzed, and when he read the message, the smile faded. He sent a text before returning the phone to his pocket.

Our waiter arrived to take our order, and after he left, I asked Romy, "Is everything alright? That text seemed to upset you."

"It's fine. That was my mom, cancelling dinner tonight because her fiancé surprised her with two tickets to a show. With everything that happened in the last twelve hours, I'd actually forgotten about our plans, so it worked out perfectly."

"Then why do you look sad?"

"I didn't realize I did. But lately…I guess I feel like I'm not much of a priority for my family. I mean, I get it. Both my mom and my brother got engaged over the past few months, and they've been spending most of their time with their new fiancés. I'm happy for them."

"But you also feel left out," I guessed.

"Or left behind, maybe. It was always the three of us, and we're really close." After a moment, he muttered, "And yes, I know how selfish I sound."

"Why do you think you sound selfish?"

"Because I'm making it about me, and it's not. Things change. We weren't going to be a family of three forever."

"It's okay to feel left behind. In fact, that's a perfectly understandable reaction."

"I know." He didn't look convinced, though.

I asked, "Have you told your family how you feel?"

"No, and I'm not going to. I don't want to cast a shadow on their happiness."

"Is that also why you haven't told them about your dad?"

He considered the question before admitting, "Maybe that's part of it."

"Do you do that a lot? Trying to shield your family from the bad things that happen in your life, because you don't want to upset them?"

"I guess so, especially with stuff I encounter at work. I've seen some things that…" Romy's voice trailed off as he sort of shrank into himself, and a pained look appeared in his eyes. "Let's just say the job can be pretty horrible and overwhelming at times."

"If it's hurting you, and it really seems like it is, why don't you quit?"

28

"Because I should be tougher than this. I'm trying to be. If only I could develop a thick skin, or a sense of detachment…"

"How long have you been an EMT?"

"Five years."

"I know you didn't ask for my opinion," I said, "but it really sounds like you need to find a different job, Romy. This one's pretty obviously hurting you, and that's not right."

"Yeah, but Reno would be so disappointed if I quit."

"Reno?"

"That's what I call my brother Adriano," he explained. "I couldn't say his name when I was little, and somehow that nickname stuck. I can't remember if I told you he's ten years older than me. In a lot of ways, he's more of a father figure than a brother, and I've always wanted him to be proud of me. He paid my tuition when I was in college, and when I told him I wanted to be an EMT, you should have seen him. He was practically bursting with pride, and that felt so good. How can I go to him after all of that and tell him I couldn't hack it?"

"You didn't just turn around and quit the minute things got hard, Romy. You've been trying to hang in there for *years*, but from the sound of it, that isn't the right job for you. If your brother can't understand that, then fuck him."

On that note, three waiters marched into the dining room with a lot of fanfare, carrying a sizzling skillet of fajitas along with tortillas, rice and beans, and a platter heaped with all the fixings. The smile returned to Romy's beautiful face, and he thanked the waiters and told them, "This looks fantastic."

While we ate, he tried to lighten the mood by telling me about some of his culinary disasters over the years. At one point, he said, "My failure as a cook goes way back. When I was nine, my mom and brother were both at work, so I decided to make myself a burrito for dinner. That should have been so simple, but I ended up setting the stove on fire and calling 911."

I got that he was going for an amusing anecdote, and I smiled appreciatively. But what I heard was a story about a lonely kid who had to grow up too fast, and it made me feel even more protective of him than I already did.

On the way back to the car after lunch, Romy froze and grabbed my hand. I thought something was wrong, and my adrenaline surged. But then he pointed and whispered, "Look over there, in the tall grass at the edge of the parking lot."

I was surprised to see a coyote standing perfectly still and watching us, mostly because it was my second time seeing one in less than twenty-four hours. It felt like a sign in a way, especially since the first one had sent me back to town and straight to Romy.

He whispered, "Isn't he beautiful?" Was he? An argument could be made that he was kind of cute, but I didn't know if I'd call him beautiful. Romy was mesmerized though, and after a moment he said, "Sometimes I get tired of living in the desert. But then it offers up a gift like this, and I'm reminded there's beauty and wonder all around us. I just have to take the time to look for it."

When the animal turned and disappeared, Romy let go of my hand and ran after it. What the hell? I'd obviously been right when I thought he had terrible instincts. Not only had he brought me home with him, but now he was running toward a wild animal, instead of away from it.

I gave chase and finally caught up to Romy when he was about ten yards into the knee-high grass. Then I asked, "What are you doing? Don't you know that's a dangerous animal?"

He turned to me with a smile, and with mischief in his eyes. "Of course I do, but he wasn't going to let me catch him." Okay, so maybe he had a point. Then he gestured at a small ravine up ahead and said, "There's a creek down there. Can we go take a look?"

"You can go anywhere you want."

"I know, but will you come with me?"

I grinned and told him, "I'll follow you anywhere. Even down a dusty hillside, to a sad little stream with a possibly rabid coyote."

Romy grinned, too. "In other words, you're really not the outdoorsy type."

"Yes and no. I try to spend most of my free time outdoors. But that's more along the lines of sitting on a balcony with a drink, not actively interacting with nature."

He chuckled at that and took my hand again. "Don't worry. If anything natural tries to actively interact with you, I'll intervene."

We made our way downhill to the creek, and it turned out I'd been right to call it sad. It just wasn't much to speak of—unless you'd grown up in the desert, apparently. Romy was almost as enthusiastic about that little trickle of water as he'd been about the coyote. He even decided he needed to go and stand in it, after taking off his shoes and socks and rolling up the cuffs of his jeans.

Meanwhile, I sat down on the remains of a rock wall and watched him as he splashed around. His genuine happiness at such a simple thing was charming.

After a few minutes, he came over to me with a big smile and said, "You should stick your feet in the creek. It feels really good."

"It's more fun to watch you."

"You could do both at the same time," he pointed out, as he pulled his hoodie off over his head. His T-shirt rode up when he did that, and the glimpse of his belly button and a few inches of skin made my heart race. How was that so unbelievably sexy? But then, everything about him was, so it shouldn't come as a surprise.

He leaned in to place the hoodie beside me on the rock wall, and when he looked up, his face was just inches from mine. Both of us became very still as he met my gaze. Then he licked his lips reflexively.

I knew he wanted me to kiss him. I wanted it too, more than anything, but my guilt held me back.

"There's a lot you don't know about me." My voice sounded so rough that I barely recognized it. "You wouldn't want me if you knew."

He touched my cheek, so gently that it made my heart ache. "I don't care about your past. All that matters is you and me, right here and now."

"Are you sure?"

Even though he nodded, I knew I should tell him I was Mario Greco. He deserved the truth. But a part of me, a desperately lonely part I usually tried to ignore, whispered, *Please, don't screw everything up. You really need this.*

While that inner debate raged, Romy searched my eyes. Then he took my face between his hands and brushed his lips to mine. The kiss was soft and tender and beautiful, and it was devastating.

I knew this thing that was starting to happen between us could only end badly. He'd find out who I was, and he'd hate me. But I couldn't think about that now. I just couldn't. Instead, I tried to quiet my mind and live in the moment.

That was overwhelming too, though. I usually didn't feel much of anything, because it was easier to go through life with a tight lid on my emotions. But without even trying, Romy had torn that lid off and thrown it aside, and now I felt everything. It was like being swept up in a strong current—I felt like I was drowning in it.

Fine. Let me drown.

He rocked his hips and rubbed his hard-on against mine. Before I could overthink it, I slid off the wall and swung us around. Then I dropped to my knees.

Usually, I was the one on the receiving end. But I wanted to give to Romy instead of taking from him, and this was one very literal way of doing that.

He let me fumble with his clothes for a few moments before taking over. As soon as he unzipped and pushed his jeans and briefs to mid-thigh, I wrapped my lips around the tip of his cock. I felt clueless and awkward as I tried to slide my mouth down his shaft. But then he murmured, "That feels good," and it encouraged me to keep going.

The blow job that followed was definitely lacking in finesse. It didn't seem to matter though, judging by the sounds he made and the fact that he was rock hard in my mouth. I was totally focused on my technique, but after a few minutes, he touched my cheek and said, "Look at me, Marcus."

The moment we made eye contact, everything changed. It finally dawned on me this wasn't about the mechanics of what I was doing. It was about Romy, and the two of us, and our connection.

His expression was pure bliss. It felt good, knowing I was causing that, and it helped me relax. Then I started to really enjoy what I was doing. In fact, it was surprisingly fun.

It occurred to me most gay men probably had that revelation a lot earlier in life. That in turn reminded me how narrow my experience had been up to this point. There was a huge difference between fucking some random person and being with a lover. I'd only ever done the former, so no wonder this thing with Romy felt brand new.

Pretty soon, he blurted, "I'm about to come." Maybe that was meant as a warning, in case I didn't want to swallow his load. I just sucked harder.

He threw his head back and shot down my throat, gritting his teeth and stifling a yell. His hands clamped down on my shoulders as he thrust into my mouth, and I gripped the backs of his thighs and brought him right to the end of his orgasm.

Afterwards, he seemed shaky as he zipped up. We sat down side-by-side, leaning against the rock wall as he caught his breath. Then he asked, "What about you?"

"Next time."

He leaned against me and murmured, "That was amazing."

"You don't have to say that. I know it took me a while to figure out what I was doing."

"Because you're usually on the receiving end of blow jobs?" When I nodded, he said, "I can see that. Actually, I was surprised when you went the other direction—not that I'm complaining." He grinned at me, and then he got up and started to put on his socks and sneakers.

I could have left it at that, but instead I admitted, "Actually, I've been celibate for the past two years. For four years before that, I only had sex with men I was paying."

When he glanced at me, I was glad to see his expression was curious instead of disgusted. "Why would a man as attractive as you pay for sex? All you'd have to do is walk into any bar or log on to an app, and you'd have men falling at your feet."

"Because if you're with a sex worker, two things are perfectly clear—you're in charge, and it's just a one-time thing with no strings or emotional attachments."

"I can understand that," he said. "So, why'd you stop?"

"Because it started making me feel lonelier than just staying home by myself and jerking off. I should probably mention I always practiced safe sex with those men, and I've been tested twice in the past two years. I'm negative across the board, so you don't have to worry. I mean, you know, if we decide to take this further." Awkward.

"For the record, I've been tested and am negative, too." He tied his hoodie around his waist as he asked, "So, what happened before that? You told me about the last six years, but I'm curious what got you to that point. I'm guessing it was a long-term relationship that went bad."

"No. Before that, I spent nearly a decade in prison."

"Just so you know, I don't automatically judge someone for breaking the law. In fact, some of the people I love aren't exactly law-abiding." He was trying to be discreet, but I knew he was referring to his brother. "Out of curiosity, what were you in for?"

"When I was nineteen, I was convicted of a double homicide and sentenced to life in prison." Before I could tell him the extremely crucial next part, he met my gaze with uncertainty in his eyes. Seeing that felt like a kick to the gut. What did I expect though, after a bombshell like that?

I blurted, "Wait. I was innocent, and I can prove it," as I got up and pulled my phone from my pocket. Then I whispered, "Please let me have a fucking signal."

I was so anxious that I mistyped my own name three times. Finally, I pulled up an old news story from the Sacramento Bee and held out the phone to him. He hesitated, but then he took it from my hand.

Since I knew how big and intimidating I was, I took a few steps back and sat down while he read the story. It was only five paragraphs, about a double murder conviction that had been overturned after almost a decade. It explained that the real perpetrator was caught in connection with another murder and confessed to several more, including the two that had sent me to prison. The article also told Romy my real last name, which was Greene. That made me feel kind of exposed, but so be it.

When he finished reading, he glanced at me and I told him, "I'm no saint. Let me make that clear. I break the law all the time, but I've never killed anyone. I wouldn't do that."

"I know you wouldn't," he said, as he handed me the phone. "Tell me what happened. This doesn't go into much detail."

"When I was nineteen and living in South Sacramento, I got pulled over for a busted tail light. While the cops were running my ID, a double homicide came in over the radio. It was about a mile away, and here I was, this punk kid with a juvie record and a bad attitude.

"They arrested me as a suspect, and later on, a witness picked me out of a lineup. That was a joke, because years later I found out the guy who'd actually committed the crime was almost twenty years older and five inches shorter than me. We didn't look alike either, aside from having dark hair.

"But based on the witness's testimony, I was brought to trial and found guilty by a jury. Never mind that I had no motive, no ties to the victims, and there was no physical evidence linking me to the crime."

I stared at the ground and continued, "I spent nine years, seven months, and twenty-two days in prison. I was just a kid when I went in. By the time I was released, I was twenty-eight. A decade of my life had been stolen from me, and there wasn't a single fucking thing I could do about it."

Romy said softly, "I'm so sorry. That's truly awful."

"Yeah, it wasn't great."

After a moment he whispered, almost under his breath, "What must that do to a person?"

I knew he wasn't really asking me, but I answered anyway. "It made me into a really bitter, hostile, pissed off asshole."

Romy shook his head. "But that doesn't describe you."

"Yes, it does. You're the only person who gets to see this side of me."

"Why do I get special treatment?"

I looked away and mumbled, "You just do."

"That's not really an answer."

How could I even begin to explain this? Badly, apparently, because I ended up saying, "I'm not enough of a monster to treat you like anything other than the sweet, beautiful angel that you are, Romy. To do anything other than that would be like…hell, I don't know, like burning down the Sistine Chapel or something."

A grin curled the corners of his mouth. "You're comparing me to the Sistine Chapel?"

"Look, you're the one who tried to make me put it into words."

I started up the hill so he wouldn't see the color rise in my cheeks, and as he followed me, he said, "Okay. But like, what part of the Sistine Chapel do I remind you of? And are you Catholic? Because I feel like that affects the context."

I glanced at him and tried to frown. The amusement that sparkled in his eyes was pretty cute, though. "No, I'm not. I think it's sacred because it contains some of Michelangelo's greatest works of art, not because it's a church. Those masterpieces aren't just beautiful. They're rare and truly something special, and they need to be cherished, protected, and treated with respect. Like you."

A huge smile spread across his face. "That just went from the goofiest analogy ever to the nicest thing anyone's ever said to me."

When we reached the car, I paused and fidgeted with the key fob. "I don't know what you thought I was before, but you just got a lot of new information about me. If you'd prefer to call off this trip and go back to Vegas, I understand. Seriously. I won't even be offended."

"I don't want to do that. Why would I, because you told me you're a criminal?"

"That'd be enough for most people."

"I'm not most people," he informed me, with a playful smirk. "In fact, I'm the Sistine Chapel of human beings. Oh hey, that's good! Remind me to have business cards printed up with that caption." I pretended to scowl at him, which made him chuckle.

Then he grew serious and told me, "I do have one question, though."

I could only imagine what it might be after all of that. I braced myself and said, "Sure. What is it?"

His smile returned as he asked, "Can I keep driving?"

I was grinning as I tossed him the keys.

5

Romy

Once we started driving again, we narrowed down our destination to San Diego. Neither of us had been there before, and we liked the idea of exploring someplace new.

Marcus researched several hotels on his phone before making a reservation for us. A few minutes after that, he fell asleep. This wasn't surprising, since he'd spent the night before on a chair at my bedside and couldn't have gotten much rest.

I snuck a look at him as I thought about all he'd told me. Given what he'd been through, it was amazing that he trusted me enough to open up. Then again, maybe it was a bit like confessing to a priest, or telling a therapist his deepest feelings—I was someone he didn't have emotional ties to, so what was the harm in being vulnerable with me? I'd done the same thing to him the night before.

Actually, it fit with him seeing this as a short-term thing—and that was definitely what he meant by telling me he couldn't promise anything beyond the next few days. We were two people who'd met at a crossroads, and our lives were traveling in different directions. It made sense that this was just for now.

Although…

I glanced at him again before returning my gaze to the open

road. Despite all my claims that I was done with relationships, I really hoped this ended up turning into more than just a quick fling. I wasn't just attracted to Marcus, I was drawn to him. And even though it was obvious we were very different people, I couldn't help but think we fit together somehow.

But I had to play it cool. It was important to go into this without a lot of expectations and just be open to whatever happened. If it was meant to be, we'd figure that out.

～

Marcus woke with a start a few hours later, looking an awful lot like he was ready to punch somebody as he blurted, "Where am I?"

Because I'd predicted this, I was sitting on a nearby bench, reading an ebook. I pocketed my phone as I explained, "We're in San Diego. Since you told me waking up in unfamiliar places feels disorienting, I decided to stop at this park for a while. It seemed like a better idea than letting you wake up at valet parking in front of the hotel."

"Good call." He climbed out of the car and stretched before joining me on the bench. "What would you have done if I'd woken up swinging while you were driving?"

"I would have pulled to the side of the road and talked you down."

"That must be your EMT training. I doubt most people would seem so calm about it." After a moment, he glanced at me and said, "I'm really sorry. I know it's weird."

"There's no need to apologize. It's not something you can control."

"No, but I should have tried harder to stay awake."

I shrugged. "You were up most of the night, so I'm glad you got some rest."

"But then you had to do all the driving, and I didn't even keep you company."

"That's fine. It gave me time to think, and I needed that."

"Were you thinking about your dad?"

As I focused on some kids climbing on a play structure across the parking lot, I said, "Yeah, for the last part of the drive. Last night was definitely upsetting, but I've realized it didn't really change anything. He made the choice to leave my mom and ignore the fact that he had a kid. I already knew that. Whether he ended up moving back east like he said he would or staying in town, the end result is the same—he didn't want me, and I didn't need him. I just have to get past the shock of realizing my dad had just died in front of me..."

When my voice trailed off, Marcus took my hand, and we sat in silence for a while. I liked the fact that he gave me time to get myself together, and that he didn't try to make me feel better with a bunch of useless platitudes.

After a while, I decided to change the subject. Processing what had happened with my dad would take time. Right now, there was no solution to be found, no thought or idea that was going to make it any easier. So I made a conscious effort to set it aside and said, "I was also thinking about what you'd told me about your time in prison. How did you survive, Marcus? You were so young when you went in, and that must have been such a hostile environment."

"At first, I survived by fighting like a rabid dog. Any time someone tried to push me, I pushed back with everything I had."

"Did it work? Did they leave you alone after a while?"

"Hell no. All I succeeded in doing was pissing off pretty much everyone. That got me beat up, stabbed twice, and nearly killed. The only reason I survived was because a man named Arturo Giannopoulos, better known as Artie the Greek, took pity on me. It turned out I reminded him of his only son, who'd been killed at twenty-three. Art took me under his wing, and from then on I was untouchable. That was the kind of power he had, both inside that prison and on the outside."

I asked, "Is he the man you referred to as your mentor?"

Marcus nodded and shifted his gaze to the grass beneath our feet. "I'd be dead if it wasn't for him. I know that for a fact. I got out four years before he died of cancer, and I kept the promise I made to him by taking over the empire he'd spent a lifetime building.

"I was the only person he trusted to carry out his wishes. It wasn't easy. It still isn't. But I owe him. He not only kept me alive, he gave me the money and resources I needed to succeed on the outside. When he died, it turned out he left me a fortune, including an art collection that's worth millions. It's not my taste at all, so I've been selling off a few pieces here and there. The challenge is finding collectors who actually appreciate it, instead of just seeing it as an investment. That's what Art would have wanted."

"It's incredible that he left you so much."

Marcus frowned. "Yeah, but there were definitely strings attached. One thing he wanted was for me to make my mark in Las Vegas. He was a New York gangster, born and bred. But when he came to Vegas, he fell in love with it, and running its criminal underground became his ultimate goal.

"The problem is, times changed while he was locked up. These days, the power is spread out across numerous gangs, mobs, individuals, and organizations, so there's no way anyone could actually take over. It's like a hydra—cut off one head, and two grow back. I made a few inroads, but even with all the resources Art left me, it was an impossible task, especially because I wasn't willing to kill anyone to show I meant business. The same can't be said for the type of people I usually dealt with."

I murmured, "That all sounds incredibly dangerous."

"It is, but it helped that rumors spread about me. People believed I was a ruthless killer, and for a while, that reputation was enough. But things started to get messy, especially when I realized I didn't have full control over my own crew. Finally, I decided to pull back and let things settle down.

"At the same time, several of Art's former associates have decided they're entitled to the money he left me and have been trying to track me down. I've managed to stay a step ahead of them, but eventually, my luck's going to run out."

I asked, "What made you return to Vegas?"

"Pride and sheer stubbornness, I guess. I'd had a run-in with someone a while back, and I just couldn't let it go." He paused for a moment. It seemed like there was more he wanted to say about that, but then he got up and changed the subject with, "Anyway, we should go find our hotel. It's probably getting close to dinnertime."

It took just a few minutes to drive to our destination, which turned out to be a luxurious resort. When I got a look at the Spanish-style buildings and lush, tropical landscaping, I whispered, "It's like something out of a movie." That made him smile.

As soon as we pulled up to the main entrance, our bags and the car were efficiently whisked away by the parking attendants. Marcus told me to have a seat once we got inside, so I made myself comfortable in the lobby while he went to reception.

I tried not to seem ridiculously unsophisticated as I took it all in, but this hotel was *nice*, in a very different way than the flashy hotels on the strip. It was going for a laid back California-casual vibe with its rattan furniture, loads of plants, and friendly staff in floral shirts, but there was no question it was extremely high-end.

Pretty soon, Marcus returned and handed me a slim, royal blue envelope embossed with a gold palm tree. "Here's your key card," he said. "Our rooms are ready, so would you like to go check them out?"

I got up and repeated, "Rooms, plural? As in, we're not staying in the same one?"

He nodded. "I thought you'd want some privacy."

That made sense, of course. We were still getting to know each other, so what did I think, that he'd booked us the honeymoon suite? He was being considerate, and that little tinge of disappointment I felt was totally unwarranted.

He led the way out the back of the building, then past a huge pool and open-air bar before pausing to look around. Finally, he gestured to the right. "I think it's that way, according to the map at reception. I didn't want a bellman to show us to our rooms, because it's annoying when they hover."

Once we found the right building, I discovered that what he called a room was actually a massive suite. "I'm going to get cleaned up," he said, after I opened my door and took a couple of steps inside. "Would you like to meet for drinks in an hour?"

I turned back to look at him and nodded. He was still out in the hallway, fidgeting with his keycard.

"I'm right next door," he told me, "and there's a connecting door between our suites. Just knock if you need anything."

"Okay. See you soon." He continued down the hall, and I closed the door behind him. Then I wandered into the living room and muttered, "Damn." My entire apartment could have fit in here, twice.

The style was similar to the lobby, with a subdued green, white, and tan color palette, along with warm wood tones. The tropical theme was carried through in colorful arrangements of exotic flowers, which were scattered throughout the room. There was also a welcome basket full of tropical fruit. I murmured, "So fancy," and plucked a pineapple out of the basket. There was no way to actually eat it, so I ended up carrying it through the suite with me.

Beyond the living room was a balcony with an infinity pool, which gave way to a sweeping view of the Pacific. Okay, that was ridiculously nice. All of this was. I was totally out of my element.

I decided to take a shower and fix myself up before Marcus came to get me, so I went into the bedroom and placed the pineapple on a round, decorative throw pillow. Well, what else was I supposed to do with it?

My bags had actually made it to the suite before I did, and they looked shabby compared to their surroundings. I scooped them up and brought them with me to the bathroom, and then I unpacked the douching kit I'd stuck in the bottom of my bag.

I had every intention of throwing myself at Marcus before dinner, and that involved a bit of prep work. After using the kit and taking a very thorough shower, I took the extra step of working a bit of lube into me. Then I finished grooming and put on the fluffy white bathrobe that was hanging beside the double sinks.

After I hid my luggage and dirty clothes in the closet, I climbed onto the king-size bed with my phone. I'd planned to read my ebook for a while, but there was a text from Pete waiting for me. It said: *I'm bored at work because the bar's super dead. Come visit me!*

I replied: *Can't, sorry. I'm out of town with a hot guy.* Then I smiled at the camera and sent a selfie, making sure to get both the crest on the robe as well as the pineapple in the shot.

The phone rang in my hand two seconds later. When I answered, Pete yelled, "I need details! What hot guy? And where are you? It looks expensive."

"I'm at a resort in San Diego. It's a long story."

"And I want to hear all of it, so start talking."

I began by telling him what had happened at work the night before, and he said, "I'm really sorry about your dad, Romy. Are you okay?"

"I'm still trying to process it, but I seem to have shifted from sad and stunned to angry—for now, anyway. It pisses me off, knowing he could have come to see me any time over the past twenty-seven years, but he never bothered."

"He was a deadbeat, just like my dad, and he didn't deserve you." I could hear Pete shifting the phone, and then he said, "So, not to brush that stuff aside—it's obviously important."

"But you're dying to hear about the hot guy," I guessed.

"I really am! When and where did you meet him? And how the hell are you on a trip with him, after less than twenty-four hours?" After I filled him in on the details, he said, "Damn. He sounds amazing."

"He is, although he already gave me the 'I can't promise anything after this' speech."

"That doesn't mean anything," Pete insisted. "It's just what guys say. Even if they think we're perfect and amazing, they always have to lead off by telling us they're not looking for a commitment. I think it's their way of covering all the bases—so, if it doesn't work out for whatever reason, they can claim they warned us."

"Well, it sucks."

"I know, but don't read too much into it. Think of it as a standard disclaimer, like the warning they put on shampoo. They know you're not going to drink it, but they still think they have to print 'for external use only' on the bottle."

"Wait, how is that relevant?"

Pete sounded mildly exasperated. "He doesn't really assume he's going to break up with you, just like the shampoo company doesn't actually think you're going to guzzle their product. They're just like, practicing due diligence, or whatever it's called."

"Okay, got it."

"You know, normally I'd be a little worried about you running off with a stranger," he said, "but this guy sounds sweet. Besides, if he was planning to murder you, he could have done it last night, while you were sleeping. And the fact that he got you your own room tells me he's respectful. I like that."

"I do too, although two suites are overkill. There are at least two bedrooms in this one, maybe three. I haven't even finished exploring all of it yet. I think we could have shared it and still maintained plenty of personal space."

"Hang on, I have a customer." I could hear him greet one of our regulars by name. After he poured her a beer, he came back on the line and we chatted for a couple more minutes. Then a few more customers came into the bar, and I promised to talk to him soon before we ended the call.

Next, I texted my brother. I started with: *I have some news. It's about my dad.*

For the second time that evening, the phone rang in my hand. When I answered, Adriano asked, "Did that asshole finally get in touch with you?"

"Not exactly."

I repeated the story yet again, and he said, "Shit, Romy, I'm sorry that happened to you. Does Mom know?"

"Not yet, because as soon as I tell her, she's going to go off on a guilt spiral. You know how she is. She'll blame herself for the fact that he was such a jerk and never came to see me, only the guilt will be much worse this time. I just can't deal with that right now."

"No, I totally get it. Want me to tell her for you?"

"Thanks for the offer, but I'll tell her. I just need a little time."

"Do you want me to come home? Jack and I were planning to return to Vegas in two weeks, but we can move some stuff around—"

"No, it's okay. I'm with a new friend. He's been great about listening and being there for me, so I'm not dealing with this alone."

"New friend as in, some guy you're dating?"

"Something like that."

Adriano tried to sound casual as he asked, "So, who is he?" He hated everyone I'd ever dated, and I knew he was gearing up to hate this person, too. But first, he was going to pretend he was open-minded and accepting.

"His name's Marcus, and I met him at mom's bar."

"So, when do I get to meet this guy?"

I really wasn't going to go into the whole thing about not promising anything beyond these next couple of days, because I knew how that'd sound to my brother. Instead, I went with, "If you promise to be nice to him, maybe we can all meet for drinks in a couple of weeks when you and your fiancé are back in town."

"I'm always nice." When I snort-laughed, he said, "What? I am."

"Bullshit, Reno. You made my last boyfriend cry."

"Yeah, but he was a douchebag, so I'm not sorry."

"You made him cry way before either you or I knew he was cheating on me," I pointed out.

"He was a douchebag from the get-go. In fact, he'd probably been that way since birth. I can totally picture him as a tiny, little baby douche, with mini designer sunglasses and the collar of his onesie popped up." That made me laugh.

Then I told him, "I need to go, but I'll talk to you soon, okay?"

"For sure. Call me if you need anything, and if this new guy steps out of line, punch him in the face for me." He was kidding. Mostly.

After we said goodbye and ended the call, I went into the bathroom and tried to style my hair. Then I checked the time and realized I only had a few minutes until Marcus came over.

I ran to the walk-in closet and searched my bags to see if I'd packed anything that might be construed as sexy.

Nope.

I hadn't even brought anything nice, so I'd be woefully underdressed if he wanted to go out to dinner. That wasn't my concern right now, though. My goal was to look hot, maybe even enticing, because I wanted Marcus bad. It wasn't like me to be this thirsty, but then again, it wasn't like me to spend time with someone that unbelievably sexy, either.

After my wardrobe failed me, I took off the robe and tried a few different poses. Putting my hands on my hips made me look like a wannabe superhero. Crossing my arms made me seem closed off and defensive. Letting my arms hang at my sides was lackluster—and okay, maybe I was overthinking things.

Should I go for it? I tried to imagine answering the door wearing nothing but a smile and felt myself blushing.

I seriously had no game. How had I ever managed to get guys into bed? Well, okay, it usually wasn't much of a challenge. Most men were horndogs who'd fuck anyone that was willing. There was zero seduction required.

It felt different with Marcus. He seemed more reserved somehow, and a lot more mature and sophisticated than the men I usually dated.

Not that we were dating…

But whatever. All I needed to do was give him a little encouragement, and I was sure he'd be into it. The heat behind our earlier kiss—not to mention that blow job, which he'd initiated—were pretty clear tip-offs that he wanted me. Even so, greeting him with my twig and berries swinging in the wind was a bit much. It might come across as desperate, instead of sexy.

Just then, there was a knock—and I was buck naked. I quickly wrapped a towel around my hips before rushing out of the bathroom.

When I opened the door connecting the suites, my breath caught. Marcus was dressed in a charcoal gray suit, which had been perfectly tailored to fit his big, muscular body. Damn. Now *that* was sexy.

He ran his gaze down the length of me, then back up again. When we made eye contact, his lips parted.

In the next instant, we were all over each other.

We stumbled into my suite, locked in a fiery kiss, and he pushed me against the wall as I grabbed at him. All it took for him to strip me was a single tug on that towel, and a shudder of pleasure ran through me. I should have felt self-conscious like this—totally naked while he was fully clothed—but instead, it made my cock throb.

I wrapped my arms and legs around him and tilted my head back, giving him full access as he licked and kissed my neck. His hard-on pressed against mine through his clothes, and I felt his body tremble with desire. I loved knowing I affected him like that.

He cupped my ass with both hands, and when he skimmed my hole with a fingertip and discovered a bit of lube, he murmured, "You got yourself ready for me."

I nodded. "I need you inside me, Marcus." He made a sound that was almost a growl before kissing me again. When he moved to dotting kisses along my jaw, I told him, "We'll need more lube."

He nipped my earlobe before stepping back enough for me to untangle myself, and grinned as he said, "Lead the way."

We joined hands and hurried across the suite. Once we got to the main bathroom, I was in such a rush that I dumped my shaving kit into the sink to find the lube. When he picked up a condom, I turned to look at him and said, "We could skip that if you wanted to. Normally, I'd be all about it, but we talked about this. We've both been tested and know we're negative, so there's no need."

"Are you sure?"

"Definitely."

We ended up going at it right there in that huge, luxurious bathroom. Over the next few minutes, I helped him strip off his clothes, in between a lot of kissing, groping, and jerking each other off. Once he was naked, he picked up the lube and said, "Turn around," as a smile played on his lips.

He worked more lube into me and slicked his cock, while I bent over and rested my elbows on the marble vanity. Then he spread my ass and pushed his tip against my hole.

Because he was so thick—and maybe because I hadn't had sex in a while—I started to get a little panicky when he met with some resistance. I whispered, "It's not going to fit," and looked at him over my shoulder.

"Do you want to stop?"

"No."

He rubbed my lower back as I concentrated on relaxing enough to let him in. At the same time, he spoke to me soothingly, offering words of encouragement. I whimpered when his tip finally slipped inside me, and I begged him, "Please go slow."

"I will. I promise."

He was so patient as he worked his way into me an inch at a time. When he was about halfway in, I panicked again and whispered, "You're too big."

"We can stop if you want to, Romy. Just say the word."

"No! Please don't stop." I barely recognized my own voice. It was small and soft, and I sounded so needy.

He murmured, "Okay," and we kept trying. I shifted a bit, widening my stance and arching my back as I rested my forehead on my folded arms. That seemed to help, and eventually I opened up enough for him to slide the rest of the way in.

I raised my head and met his gaze in the mirror when he bottomed out, and he smiled at me and said, "I knew you could do it, baby." That was nice to hear.

Marcus ramped up gradually, slowly sliding in and out a few times before he finally started fucking me. Then his cock began grazing my prostate, and everything shifted. As pleasure replaced discomfort, I started driving myself back to meet each thrust. That prompted him to fuck me harder, which amplified the waves of pleasure that were rolling through me.

As I braced myself with one hand splayed against the mirror, I mumbled, "Feels so good." I looked up as he took me harder still, and what I saw made my cock throb. I'd never watched myself get fucked before, and it was a huge turn-on.

At the same time, I marveled at the way both of us were transformed. I looked flushed and wild and uninhibited, panting as I drove myself onto the thick cock in my ass. And Marcus was the sexiest thing I'd ever seen—pure strength and power as he grasped my hips and thrust into me.

When he met and held my gaze, it all became even more intense. I almost didn't know what to do with everything I felt in that moment.

But then he grasped my achingly hard cock and started jerking me off, and my focus shifted to the orgasm both of us were chasing. A minute later I cried out, thrusting my hips as I began to come. When he wrapped an arm around my chest, I grabbed onto it, as if it was the only thing keeping me from breaking into a million pieces.

Then he was coming too, slamming into my ass as a primal growl rumbled in his chest. My body shook, and I was barely aware of the fact that words were spilling from me. It sounded like someone else was repeating Marcus's name and begging, "Make me yours."

As all of that intense pleasure finally began to ebb, two things happened—a million emotions rushed in to fill the void left in its wake, and my legs gave out. Fortunately, Marcus had a strong grip on me, and he eased us both into a sitting position on the fluffy white bathmat before I could collapse.

With the last of my energy, I climbed onto him, straddling his lap as I buried my face in his shoulder. I was trembling, so he dragged his suit jacket over and wrapped it around me. As he held me securely, he asked, "Are you alright, baby?" I nodded, but he said, "Please look at me."

I raised my head and looked into his eyes. I hadn't been sure of their color until now, but in this light I saw they were pearl gray, edged in charcoal. His brows knit with concern, and he caressed my cheek as he asked, "Are you sure you're okay?"

"I'm fine." My voice sounded rough. Had I been yelling? "That was just overwhelming. I'm not used to sex being that—"

"Intense."

"Exactly." Then he kissed me, and it was so tender that it made my heart do some kind of odd little flip-flop.

After we rested for a while, Marcus cleared his throat and said, "We should get cleaned up. Do you need a hand?"

"No thanks, I've got it." To prove I could fend for myself, I climbed off his lap and stood up. I had to steady myself by leaning against the edge of the vanity, but at least my legs didn't buckle. Because I felt like I'd just run a marathon, I asked, "Can we stay in tonight and order room service? I don't really feel like going anywhere."

Marcus got up too, gathering his clothes as he mumbled, "Sure. Anything you want. I'll see you in a few minutes."

When he paused to look at me, there was wonder in his eyes. There was no other word for it. I grinned at him, and he flashed me a quick, self-conscious smile before hurrying out of the bathroom.

I watched him go, and once he was out of earshot, I whispered, "Wow."

6

Marcus

I rushed back to my suite naked, with my clothes and shoes in my arms. When I reached the main bedroom, I came to an abrupt stop and looked around. Everything felt off-kilter. It was as if the entire world had shifted over the last hour, and now nothing would ever be the same.

I didn't understand what had just happened. Sex was never like that. It was just a way to feel good and blow off some steam. But *that* —that had been something brand new.

And Romy...my god, Romy. He was sweet and achingly beautiful and an absolute wonder. I never knew men like him actually existed.

He scared the shit out of me.

I'd spent my whole life building nice, big, solid walls around myself. They were there for a *reason*, damn it. But he'd walked right through them, as if they were made of wet tissue paper.

He was going to be the death of me—probably literally, because I already knew I wouldn't be willing to walk away from him at the end of this trip. That meant his brother or one of his other gangster relatives were going to find out about us, shoot me, and bury me in the desert.

That alone should have been enough to keep me away from Romy, but it made no difference.

Also, how the hell was I supposed to tell him I was Mario Greco, after what we'd just shared? Not that I'd had any idea sex with him was going to be so life-altering.

And now, the only way for this to end was in a huge disaster. It wasn't just that he was going to be furious and hate me when he found out the truth. It was going to hurt him, which was the very last thing I wanted. Fuck, I already hated myself enough for both of us.

Just then, my phone beeped. I had to dig through the bundle of clothes in my arms to find it. The message was from a man who'd been a part of my Vegas crew, until I'd fired all of them a couple months ago. They'd had it coming, after going totally overboard while I was out of town and taking the shit with Adriano Dombruso way too far.

The message said: *A couple associates of Artie the Greek are looking for you. Guess they heard you got ahold of Artie's assets, and they want a piece of the pie. This isn't a heads-up— you're a prick and can rot in hell, but I told them I'd get the message to you. I hope they find you and kill you.*

Why the hell was that guy so pissed off? I'd hired him and the rest of the crew to do a job—to have my back and complete the tasks I assigned to them, in exchange for a very lucrative salary. When they proved to be a bunch of loose cannons by doing shit like smashing up the bar Romy's mom owned, we parted ways. End of story. I didn't owe them anything, so what the fuck was he so mad about?

Not that it should matter, except that he was dangerous and unpredictable, and I wouldn't put it past him or the rest of my former crew to decide to come after me. Like I needed more enemies.

That shit about Art's associates trying to track me down—and getting damn close, since they were speaking to my former employees—was bad news, too. Before this, they'd stuck to the east coast and had seemed unaware of my ties to Vegas. That had obviously changed.

I always knew stepping in as Art's heir would paint a target on my back. Any time large sums of money were involved, people were going to come out of the woodwork looking to grab a piece of it for themselves. I'd managed to stay ahead of Art's enemies—and former friends, for that matter—in the two years since he died, but now it felt like a noose was starting to tighten around my neck.

I couldn't deal with any of that right now, though. Romy was going to come looking for me any minute, and I was standing here naked and shivering. I had to get my shit together for his sake.

After a quick shower, I spent a minute or two trying to get my hair to look decent before going to get dressed. I put on a clean pair of briefs and was zipping my jeans when I heard a knock and a soft, "Hello?"

I went into the living room and found Romy fidgeting on his side of the open connecting door. He looked cuddly in his gray sweat pants and huge T-shirt, and I had to fight the urge to scoop him into my arms.

He started to say, "I can go away if you need more time, or—"

"No, come in. I'm going to make myself a drink. Would you like one?"

"Sure. I'll have whatever you're having."

He followed me to the bar cart in the corner. It turned out he was more confident about initiating contact than I was, so while I poured a couple of whiskeys, he ran his hands down my back.

I felt him hesitate when he got to a jagged scar just above my waistband, three inches to the left of my spine. He traced the area around it gingerly as he murmured, "That looks like…"

Part of me wanted to deny it, because I had a feeling it would upset him. But as an EMT who must have seen all kinds of shit on the job, he probably knew exactly what it was, so I told the truth. "Remember when I said I was stabbed in prison? That's one of them." I turned to him with two glasses in my hands and indicated a scar on my ribcage. "This is the other."

Romy frowned as he took the drink I offered him. "Someone literally stabbed you in the back."

"They did. The good news is, both of those handmade shanks were on the short side, so neither did much damage."

He searched my face and said, "You must have been so scared while you were in prison."

"Yeah, at first, but I grew up while I was inside. I got stronger, physically and mentally, and eventually, the fear went away. It was replaced with—" Did I really want to tell him this? It wasn't exactly flattering.

"With what?"

"Rage." Why sugar coat it? He should know that about me.

He tilted his head as he studied me. "But not anymore, right? Not since you got out?"

"I'm still fueled by anger. Sometimes, I want to burn the whole world down."

"Really?"

That was the absolute truth, but I tried to take the edge off it with an attempt at a joke. "I'd toast marshmallows on the embers." With that, I clinked my glass to his and tossed back the whiskey.

He finished his drink too, and we both set aside our glasses as he told me, "I can't decide if you're kidding."

I grinned a little. "Only about the marshmallows. I'm not a fan."

"Well, I'd probably be pretty angry too, if I'd been wrongly imprisoned for a decade." Romy moved closer and tucked his head into the curve between my neck and shoulder. Then he whispered, "If I had one wish, I'd go back in time and make sure you never got arrested."

"You shouldn't waste your wish on me, baby. I mean, sure, what happened to me sucked, and I would've loved to avoid it. But I was already pretty fucked up when I went in, so it's not like I'd be an upstanding member of society now if I'd never been locked up."

"But you were just a kid when you went in. It wasn't fair." He sounded like he was on the verge of tears.

I tried to find something positive to say about my time in prison, for his sake. "It wasn't all bad. I'd dropped out of high school, and while I was locked up I took classes and got my diploma. I also developed a love of reading and began educating myself on everything from math and science to history and literature. I'm pretty sure that never would have happened on the outside."

While I was talking, I draped my arms over his shoulders and started idly playing with the hair at the nape of his neck, which was just barely long enough to curl upward. Meanwhile, he nuzzled against my chest. The effortless intimacy between us was unlike anything I'd ever experienced. But then, that could be said for all of this.

He looked up at me and asked, "Are you trying to make me feel better about your wrongful imprisonment?"

"Yes."

"Why?"

"Because I don't want you to be upset."

Romy kissed my cheek and told me, "You're so sweet, Marcus." He was the only person on earth who'd ever say that.

I was horrified to feel myself blushing, so I let go of him and looked around as I asked, "Are you hungry? I am, so we should order dinner."

He grinned at me. "You suck at taking compliments and are clearly changing the subject, but sure. I'm hungry, too."

We found the room service menu and got comfortable on the couch. He began to study it like there'd be an exam later as he murmured, "There are too many choices, and a lot of this stuff sounds really fancy. The prices are outrageous, too. Seventeen dollars for a small salad! Not that I want a salad, but still."

"Please don't worry about the cost. Just get whatever you want."

He flipped a couple of pages and his eyes lit up as he said, "That sounds good." But then he frowned and muttered, "Never mind. It's on the children's menu."

"So what? If there's something you want on there, then get it."

Romy glanced at me. "I don't want you to think I'm an unsophisticated shlub."

"I'd never think that. What sounded good to you?"

"The grilled cheese sandwich and fries."

"Great, then that's what I'm ordering for you." I took the menu from him and scanned the page it was open to. "I'll get myself the kids' macaroni and cheese. That sounds delicious."

"It'll probably be a small portion."

"Then I'll get two of them. Now, let's see what's for dessert."

I turned to the last page and moved closer to him, so we could both read the menu. "I know you don't usually eat like this," he said. "Not with that body."

"I don't, but I'm on my first real vacation ever, so why not indulge? And speaking of indulgences, which dessert sounds good to you?"

He chewed his lower lip as he studied the menu. Finally, he said, "I can't decide. They all sound amazing."

I picked up the phone on the end table and pushed the button for room service. When someone answered, I ordered our dinner, added two cokes, and said, "Please also bring us one of everything from the dessert menu."

Romy audibly gasped and shook his head. When I glanced at him, he whispered, "It's too much! The cheapest dessert on that menu is fifteen dollars."

I turned my attention back to the person on the phone and asked her, "Are there any special request desserts that aren't included on the menu?" After I listened to her reply, I said, "Perfect. Please also add half a dozen chocolate-dipped strawberries."

Once I completed the order and hung up, Romy said, "We'll never eat all that."

"Between the two of us? Sure we will."

He leaned against me and took my hand. "I'm not used to being spoiled like that. Thank you."

"My pleasure."

"While we wait for our food, tell me something about you, Marcus."

"Like what?"

"I don't know…what's your favorite movie?"

"I don't have one."

He turned his head to look at my profile and asked, "Because there are too many awesome ones to choose from?"

I shifted a bit so I could see his face. "Because I haven't seen very many."

"Really? I probably watch ten movies a week. Granted, a lot of those are repeats. I love to come home from work and unwind with a comfort rewatch."

"So, what's your favorite?"

He shifted his gaze and began fidgeting with the hem of his shirt. "You're going to think I'm a dork if I tell you the truth. I should make up a cooler answer, like *Fight Club*."

"I'm not going to judge you for what you like. Please tell me."

"Okay. My favorite movie is *Up*."

"Is that its full name? Just *Up*?"

He looked surprised. "You've never heard of it?"

"No. When was it released?"

"In 2009." As he filled in the blanks, he murmured, "I guess you were in prison then."

"Yeah, I was."

"Not that it's a movie you would have watched anyway. I was thirteen when it came out, so you must have been about twenty. You're thirty-four now, right? I tried to do the math, based on some of the stuff you've told me."

"That's right."

I got up and opened a cabinet, which housed a large TV. As I returned to the couch with the remote and pulled up the On Demand search bar, Romy said, "You're not looking for it, are you?"

"I am. Let's watch it after dinner."

"I can name at least fifty movies you'd probably enjoy more than that one."

"But it's your favorite, so I'm curious about it." When I typed in the name, an image of a house and a bunch of balloons appeared on the screen. I asked, "Is it a cartoon?"

"It's animated."

I grinned at the slightly offended way he made that distinction. "Noted." After I cued up the movie and set aside the remote, I shifted around to face Romy. He was frowning, so I told him, "You look upset. We don't have to watch this movie if you don't want to. I just thought—"

"It's not that. I was just thinking about all you missed during those ten years. How much news reached you from the outside world while you were locked up?"

"Very little. I don't know what it's like at different levels, but I was in a maximum security prison, so everything was tightly controlled. Maybe it would have been different if I'd had visitors during that time, because they might have told me what was going on in the world. I didn't though, so it kind of felt like living on another planet, almost totally cut off from this one."

I shifted a bit to get more comfortable as I continued, "Not that that decade is still a mystery to me. I've been out for six years, so I'm up to speed on a lot of things. But with pop culture, there's really no way to catch up on all of it."

Romy's eyes were full of emotion as he asked, "No one visited you?"

I moved closer and took his hand. "It's all in the past. Don't let it upset you." I tried to change the subject with, "So, tell me, what are some must-see movies I should know about? You can be my pop culture advisor."

That turned out to be a topic he was passionate about. At one point, he ran to find a notepad and a pen, so he could make a list for me. He then proceeded to fill several sheets with scribbled notes while he raved about one film after another.

Romy might have gone on for hours—and I would have gladly listened, because I loved seeing him so excited—but the arrival of our dinner interrupted him. After I signed the bill, I told the waiter I'd take it from there and wheeled the cart into the suite.

We decided to eat on the couch, and Romy helped me move all the dishes to the coffee table. I raised a cloche and found his grilled cheese sandwich, and he thanked me as I put it in front of him. Then I removed another lid and blurted, "Holy shit!"

Romy leaned over to take a look at what I'd uncovered, and then he burst out laughing. That was the first time I'd heard it in its full glory, and it made me chuckle. He laughed with his whole body, flinging himself back onto the couch as he shrieked and howled. When he finally got it under control, he sat up and wiped tears from his eyes as he reminded me, "Well, you did order off the children's menu."

The pasta in my macaroni and cheese consisted of round discs with smiley faces punched out, which was both disturbing and hilarious. I stabbed one with a fork and sniffed it before putting it in my mouth, and Romy asked, "How is it?"

"It tastes funny." He didn't know if I was kidding for a moment, until I flashed him a smile and ate another happy face. Then he grinned delightedly and tucked into his sandwich.

After the main course, I uncovered all twelve desserts, arranged them on the coffee table, and handed Romy a fork. "This all looks wonderful," he said. "Where do we start?"

I rubbed my chin and pretended to give that question serious thought. "There are several arguments to be made here. You could start light and end rich," I said, as I gestured from a bowl of berries with whipped cream to a thick slice of cheesecake. "Or maybe the opposite approach makes sense to you. Me? I'm going straight for the chocolate." I scooped a bit of chocolate cake onto my fork and popped into my mouth, and Romy grinned and followed my lead.

Then he said, "Thank you, Marcus. I feel like a king."

"Good. That's how you should feel, every day of your life." I picked up a chocolate dipped strawberry and offered it to him. Instead of taking it from me, he leaned in and took a bite. Then he grinned as he wiped some juice from his lip with the back of his hand. "That was supposed to be flirty, but I think it ended up more like feeding a goat at a petting zoo."

I chuckled and set aside the rest of the strawberry. Then I raised his chin with a light touch and told him, "It's definitely not that second thing." After I kissed him, I murmured, "You taste so sweet."

"It's the strawberry."

"No, it isn't."

I kissed him again, and he climbed onto my lap and ended up staying there while we finished dessert. Some of the fruit and a couple of mini pies survived because we finally had to admit defeat, but he just shrugged and said, "We can have them for breakfast."

Then we got ready to watch the movie, which involved several steps, according to Romy. He turned off the lights, dragged in a comforter and some pillows from the bedroom, and would only let me hit play once we were totally settled in. We ended up on opposite ends of the couch, with our feet meeting in the middle under the big blanket.

The movie started out very cute. But then, about ten minutes in, I sat up straight and exclaimed, "Wait—did that character just *die*?"

"Yeah, but keep watching."

"What the hell! I was just starting to care about them. What kind of messed up Disney snuff film is this?"

Romy sat up and reached for the remote as he said, "I have to wind it back. You're talking over everything."

"Nothing's happening, because their partner is *dead*. And they never even made it to South America!"

He paused the film and asked, "Are you crying?"

"No." I quickly wiped my eyes, which might have been slightly damp.

"Aw, yes you are." He shifted around so we were curled up together on my end of the couch and kissed my cheek before saying, "Don't worry, it gets happier."

"Because their spouse isn't dead after all?"

"Nope, no one miraculously un-dies. It was important to the story, though."

"That's cold. Also, how is this your favorite movie? It's fucking depressing."

Romy tried to look stern, but he was clearly fighting back a grin as he asked, "Are you done complaining so we can keep watching?"

"I guess."

Once we both got settled, nestled together this time like a pair of spoons, he pressed play. Fortunately, the movie took a major upswing a few minutes later. Some parts of it were actually very funny. There was a bit toward the end with a scrapbook that made me tear up again, but overall, it turned out to be a surprisingly good movie.

When it ended, Romy sat up and turned to look at me as he asked, "Did you like it?"

My answer was clearly important to him. He'd just shared something that mattered to him, and it seemed like he was hoping for my approval. I drew him into my arms and said, "It was wonderful. Thank you for sharing it with me." He looked relieved as we curled up again. "So, tell me. What makes that your favorite movie, among the hundreds you've watched?"

He thought about it before saying, "When the movie first came out, I guess I identified with Russell. He was this dorky, earnest kid with an absentee dad, and he tried so hard to do the right thing, and...I don't know. That character just spoke to me.

"Then there was the wonder of it—flying off on a big adventure with a million balloons, how great is that? And at its heart, it's such a beautiful love story. Who doesn't want a love like the one Carl and Ellie shared?"

"I'm glad I asked," I said, "because that tells me a lot about you."

"Yeah? Like what?"

"For one thing, you're a hopeless romantic."

"Not hopeless," Romy told me with a grin. "I was, for a while there. But now...now I'd have to say I'm back to being hopeful."

We spent the next few hours talking about light subjects like movies and books. When Romy's lids started to get heavy, I nuzzled his cheek and told him, "We should probably think about going to bed."

"This was such a good day," he mumbled drowsily. "I don't want it to end."

"It was the best day of my life." I meant that. "Just think though, tomorrow's a brand new day."

"What should we do tomorrow?"

"Anything you want."

"The zoo? It's supposed to be incredible." He was so tired that his words were starting to slur.

"Of course, baby."

I got up and gathered him into my arms, and he whispered, "Stay with me, Marcus. Sleep in my bed with me, so we can wake up together."

"You know that's a bad idea, Romy. I'm going to freak out when I wake up in an unfamiliar place. What if I lash out at you before I'm fully awake?"

"I'll take my chances. Please? I want you to hold me."

How could I say no to that? Maybe I could stay awake all night. It was definitely worth a try.

I tucked him into bed and dropped my jeans onto the floor before sliding under the covers with him. He was almost asleep, but he reached for me with both hands. We curled around each other, and I breathed in his clean scent.

I never knew it was possible to feel this good, or be this happy.

7

Romy

I woke up in Marcus's arms, with a vague recollection of begging him to stay with me the night before. He was still asleep, and it occurred to me I should probably slip out of bed, just in case he freaked out when he woke up in an unfamiliar setting.

But I ended up lingering because I was so warm and comfortable, and pretty soon he murmured, "Romy."

He drew me closer, and after a few moments, I asked, "Are you awake?"

"Mostly." His voice was deep and rough.

I grinned and told him, "You didn't freak out when you woke up, even though you were someplace unfamiliar."

He mumbled, as he nuzzled my hair, "I wasn't someplace unfamiliar. I was with you." I thought that was amazing. Did it mean he was already so comfortable with me that I'd become his safe place? "I meant to stay awake," he added, "just to avoid doing something ridiculous when I woke up. Obviously, I failed at that."

"Good. I'm glad you got some rest."

He kissed my forehead before climbing out of bed. "I'm going in search of my toothbrush. Then I'll see about ordering us some coffee."

Marcus picked up his jeans on the way out of the bedroom, and I stared at his ass in those little black briefs until he was out of sight. I was grinning as I rolled out of bed and started my day.

We went to the zoo right after breakfast and ended up spending the entire day there. I loved the way Marcus completely dropped his tough guy façade and let himself act as dorky as I did. He'd never been to a zoo before, and he spent the entire visit in a state of wonder. He was great about indulging me, too. That included letting me spend all the time I wanted with the giraffes, which were my favorite animals.

About twenty minutes before the zoo closed, we finally headed toward the exit. But on the way out, Marcus spotted the gift shop and said, "I want to buy you a souvenir." He then selected the biggest stuffed giraffe they had, which was about five feet tall. When he saw me looking at some T-shirts with giraffes on them, he said, "Pick out your favorite and I'll get you that, too."

"Are you sure? That stuffed animal is probably expensive."

"I don't care about the cost." He sounded sincere when he told me, "I'd buy you everything in here if I thought it'd make you happy."

When I picked out a blue shirt, he frowned—very slightly, but I still caught it, so I asked, "Don't you like this one?"

"The shirt's cute. It's just that you selected the biggest one you could find. I don't mean to sound critical, I swear. I'm just trying to understand why you wear your shirts four sizes too big."

"Habit, I guess. I was really scrawny until I was about twenty, and I was so self-conscious about it that I hid my body in baggy clothes. I knew I had to get stronger for my job, so I started going to the gym and filled out some. But I guess I still see myself as that skinny, awkward kid."

"I wish you could see yourself through my eyes," he said, as he gently ran his hand down my arm. "To me, you're absolute perfection, Romy. If you like the XXL shirt and feel comfortable in it, then that's absolutely the one we'll buy. But for the record, you're gorgeous and sexy, and you have an extraordinarily beautiful body."

I searched his eyes, because I almost wondered if he was kidding. None of those were words I'd ever apply to myself. He looked completely serious, though.

After a moment, I returned the big shirt to the rack and selected the same style in my size. He smiled at me and said, "I'm proud of you."

"What makes you say that?"

"Because it takes a lot of courage to stop hiding."

On the way to the register, he kept plucking more things from the shelves for me—candy, a baseball cap, some little tchotchkes. Then I spotted something and said, "I'll meet you outside." When he was busy checking out, I took a little item to another register. It didn't look like much, especially given the huge haul he was buying me, but I hoped he'd appreciate the sentiment behind it.

When we met up at some benches in front of the gift shop, I put his present in his hand and said, "I wanted you to have something to remember today."

He took a look at the pewter keychain, which was in the shape of two giraffes leaning into each other with their necks crossed. His eyes were bright with unshed tears when he met my gaze, and he said, "Thank you. I'll never forget today, and I'll cherish this." It was such a little thing, so to see how much it touched him made my heart ache. He obviously wasn't used to people doing nice things for him.

As was usually the case when he showed a lot of emotion, Marcus seemed embarrassed. He put the keychain in his pocket and picked up the shopping bags as he changed the subject with, "I don't know about you, but I'm starving. When we get to the car, maybe you can use your phone to find us a restaurant."

I hoisted the stuffed giraffe onto my shoulder and, "Will do."

We ended up going with a nearby sushi restaurant. After dinner I told him, as we walked back to the car hand-in-hand, "I had so much fun today."

"Me, too."

When we reached the Porsche, I turned to him and said, "We'd initially mentioned staying here for a couple of days, and I know you're busy and all, but do you think we could maybe stay a little longer? I hate the thought of this coming to an end and heading back to Vegas so soon."

Marcus grinned and admitted, as he opened the car door for me, "When I made our reservation, I booked the suites for a week."

"That's great! I'm curious though, why didn't you tell me?"

"I knew you had the week off, but I had no idea how this was going to go. I didn't want you to feel obligated to stick around that long if you weren't into it."

He grinned when I told him, "I'm definitely into it." Then I asked, as I slid into the passenger seat, "Do you feel like going out and doing something else before we head back to the hotel?"

"What did you have in mind?"

"Maybe it'd be fun to go out dancing and have a few drinks. I looked it up earlier, and we're close to Hillcrest. There are several gay bars in that neighborhood."

I really thought he'd need convincing, but Marcus just said, "Sure. Anything you want, baby."

Two hours and a couple of tequila shots later, both of us were working up a sweat on the dance floor in a pretty high-energy bar. For someone who said he never danced, Marcus had a lot of natural rhythm, and I loved the way he moved.

I felt bold enough to take off the baggy flannel shirt I'd worn all day, leaving me in a form-fitting tank top and jeans. This was entirely unlike me, but he'd built up my confidence with all the complimentary things he'd said about my appearance, so I wanted to look sexy for him.

He seemed appreciative, too, judging by the way his gaze kept sweeping up and down my body. It was a huge ego boost. So was the fact that I was with the sexiest man in that bar, and he only had eyes for me.

Once we finally stepped off the dance floor, both of us were pretty overheated. I fanned myself with my hand, and Marcus said, "I'll get us some water."

"I'm going to find the restroom while you do that. I'll meet you back here in a couple of minutes."

I worked my way through the crowd and headed down the hallway at the back of the building, but I never reached my destination. Instead, I was intercepted by a blond, drunk douchebag, who was easily six-foot-five and solid muscle. He tried to grab my ass as he said, "You're cute. Come home with me."

"Yeah, I don't think so."

When I tried to step around him, he pushed me against the wall and leaned into me as he slurred, "Come on, don't play hard to get. I know you want it." I could smell beer, whiskey, and garlic as he breathed into my face. It made me want to gag.

I was half a second from kneeing him in the nuts to get him off me, but all of a sudden that big jerk was airborne. He crashed into the door at the end of the hall, which swung open, dumping him into an alley.

Marcus strode after the douche, hauled him to his feet by the front of his shirt, and slammed him into a dumpster. "He's mine," Marcus hissed, shaking the guy like he was a rag doll. "Do you hear me? Mine!"

I ran outside after them, and damned if that caveman shit didn't make my cock throb. The drunk douchebag tried to take a swing at Marcus, who effortlessly ducked that meaty fist. Then he picked the guy up like a professional wrestler and tossed him into the dumpster. A few people had followed us outside, and at that, they sent up a chorus of cheers, applause, and laughter.

When Marcus turned to me, he looked absolutely lethal. His eyes were blazing, and his jaw was set in a hard line. I'd never seen this side of him, and it was. Sexy. As. Fuck. His hands were balled into fists at his sides, and he shook them out as he mumbled, "Sorry, Romy. That was—"

He never got to finish his sentence, because I grabbed him with both hands and crushed my lips to his. Then I whispered in his ear, "I need your cock in my mouth, as soon as possible."

He looked surprised, but then a grin spread across his face. "Like I said before, anything you want, baby."

One of the waiters appeared just then and handed me my shirt and Marcus's jacket as he said, "I figured you were probably done after that and would want your stuff." After I thanked him, he said, "No, thank you and your boyfriend. That big, blond asshole grabbed my ass so many times tonight, I lost count. I'm glad someone finally took out the trash."

From inside the dumpster, the douchebag muttered, "It smells like used cheese in here."

I burst out laughing, and then I grabbed Marcus's hand and ran down the alley with him. Along the way, I told him, "For the record, I was just about to introduce my kneecap to his junk when you showed up. I'm not helpless. That said, it was damn hot to see you in full protector mode."

"I know you can take care of yourself. But when I saw that fucker touching you, I went ballistic. Not that I had any right to call you mine, or to get so territorial."

"But I *am* yours," I said, as we reached the Porsche. "That's been true since the first time you kissed me."

He muttered, "Fuck, Romy," and pushed me against the car door before claiming my mouth in a deep kiss.

We'd parked the car on a quiet side street, and the top was up because I didn't want anyone to steal my giraffe while we were gone. It wasn't totally private, but it would do. Once he got the door open and tumbled into the passenger seat, I climbed on top of him and kissed him again while he cupped my ass with both hands.

After a moment, I climbed over the gear shift and knelt on the driver's seat, and then I reached back and turned the giraffe around, so he was facing the back of the car. "Don't watch, Mr. Raffers," I joked. "It's about to get nasty in here."

Marcus pretended to look shocked. "Is it?"

"You know it is," I said, as I unfastened his belt.

The blow job that followed was messy, urgent, and so much fun. It was really gratifying to listen to his gasps and stifled moans, and to feel the way his body trembled when I did something he particularly liked.

At one point, a group of guys walked right past us with whistles and cat-calls, but I didn't even pause. I figured the windows were too fogged up for them to see much anyway, and even if they caught a glimpse, so what? Nobody knew me here, so if I wanted to be wild for once in my life, what was the harm?

After a few minutes, Marcus bit back a yell and shot down my throat. It seemed to go on for a while. Finally, he collapsed against the seat, gasping for air.

I pulled up his briefs and said, "I'll drive while you gather your energy. Just so you know, round two begins the minute we get back to our hotel." He handed me the keys and smiled at me before going back to panting and sweating.

As promised, we picked up right where we left off the moment we reached my suite. I slammed him against the back of the door as he pulled my shirt over my head, and we kissed frantically before racing each other to the bedroom.

Clothes went flying, and as soon as we tumbled onto the mattress, my cock was in his mouth. I was so turned on that it only took a matter of minutes for him to make me come, using his hand and mouth in tandem.

Now it was my turn to collapse in a heap and gasp for air. Marcus looked like he was pretty proud of himself as he stretched out at my side and waited for me to recover. When I shivered, he pulled a blanket over both of us, and I curled up in his arms.

Once I caught my breath, I told him, "Today was another absolutely astonishing day. How am I supposed to go back to reality after this? It'll probably feel like getting cast out of the Garden of Eden."

Marcus held me securely and said, "Let's try not to worry about that. We decided to stay in San Diego for a week, and I'd love it if we could just ignore the real world until we leave here. There's going to be all kinds of shit waiting for us on the other side. But for right now, we have this, and I don't want anything to screw it up." I nodded in agreement.

Eventually, we got up long enough to get cleaned up, brush our teeth, and get ready for bed. Then we met back under the covers, dressed only in briefs. I'd brought my phone along so I could plug it in on the nightstand, but first, I pressed my cheek to Marcus's and snapped a selfie.

When I showed him the photo, he grinned and said, "Cute. Send me a copy. But please keep it private, okay?"

"Don't worry, I will." I knew he broke the law, just like my brother. I also knew he might have enemies who'd love to track him down, so I understood the importance of not posting his name or photo on social media. I assumed that was what he meant.

He typed his name and number into my phone because I didn't actually have it, and I sent him the photo. Then I plugged the phone in and rolled onto my side, so I was facing him. He got in the same position with a hand tucked under his head, and I asked, "What do you think we should do tomorrow?"

"Stay in bed all day and fuck."

I grinned and nodded. "Good plan. Maybe the day after that, we can go to the animal safari, or whatever it's called."

"What's that?"

"I think it's kind of like a zoo, but the animals aren't in enclosures and they drive you through in a truck, like you're on safari. I could be wrong, though. Also, I realize we just spent about eight hours at a zoo today. If you're sick of seeing animals, we really don't have to go and do that safari thing."

"No, I want to. And I loved today. I can hardly believe I saw real elephants, giraffes, and lions. It was amazing."

"It's surprising that you'd never been to a zoo before, although this was only my second time. My brother took me to L.A. for the weekend when I was about ten or eleven, and we visited the zoo and the La Brea tar pits, and a bunch of other cool stuff. My mom wanted to take me, but she was working seven days a week at that point to try to make ends meet."

"That must have been hard for her."

"For sure. There's really nothing easy about being a single mom, but I guess you know that."

"What makes you say that?"

"You mentioned Art was the closest thing you had to a dad," I said. "I assumed that meant you were raised by a single mom, like I was."

"Actually, I spent most of my childhood in foster care."

"I'm sorry. Are you an orphan?" I shouldn't have asked, and as soon as the words were out of my mouth I regretted it. There were all kinds of ways a kid could end up in foster care, and none of them were good. It was also none of my business.

But he said, "No. I was taken away from my parents when I was six, because..." He paused and broke eye contact. After a moment he whispered, "Because they hurt me."

My heart shattered, and I whispered, "Oh god, Marcus—"

I'd started to tell him how sorry I was, but he cut me off by lightly pressing a finger to my lips. "Please don't make a big deal of it," he said, as he met my gaze again. There was so much pain in his eyes, but he was making a real effort to keep his expression neutral. "I don't want your pity, and I don't want to talk about it. I just...I wanted you to know. Eventually, I want you to know everything about me. But if there are things I hold back at first...please just know I have my reasons."

"Of course."

He sat up and said, "I'm not tired yet, are you?"

"Not really."

"Want to do another movie night? We can order popcorn and candy from room service and watch another of your favorites."

I got it. He'd shared a bit more than he was comfortable with, and now he really needed to steer the evening back onto solid ground. "Great idea," I said, as I climbed out of bed. "We can go in a totally different direction with our movie choice. Hey, have you seen *Alien?*"

"No," he said, as he followed me to the living room. "I've heard of it, though. It's supposed to be cute, right?"

I flashed him a smile. "I'm not sure what film you're thinking of, but let's just say cute doesn't quite sum it up."

8

Romy

That entire week at the resort was perfection. Some days were spent going out and exploring San Diego. Others were spent in bed, exploring each other.

It was hard to imagine getting back to real life after this. Marcus and I hadn't really discussed what we'd do next, because he was determined to live in the moment. But after this magical week, I knew we'd be leaving here as a couple.

On the afternoon of our last full day in San Diego, I was out on the patio, reading an ebook on my phone while Marcus visited the resort's gift shop. As soon as he returned, I fully intended to coax him back into bed. We'd already had sex twice that day, but I just couldn't get enough of him.

A message from Pete popped onto my screen, which said: *Hey, Romy. I hadn't heard from you in a few days, so I wanted to check in. How's life in paradise?*

I replied: *It's been amazing. Sorry I've been out of touch.*

He wrote: *No worries, I totally understand. If I was holed up in a luxury resort with a hot guy, I can guarantee I'd be out of touch, too. So, is it official? Is he your boyfriend now?*

I replied: *He is as far as I'm concerned, but we haven't discussed it or anything.*

Pete's next message said: *Sometimes you don't need to discuss it, because it just happens. Also, do I get to see a pic of this hottie, or what? I'm super curious about him.*

I scrolled through the photos I'd taken throughout the week and landed on the first selfie I'd snapped of the two of us. Marcus had wanted me to keep it private, but I assumed he'd been asking me not to post it to social media. What could be the harm in showing my friend?

About two seconds after I sent the photo, my phone rang in my hand. Pete's name was on the screen, and when I answered, I expected him to start gushing about how gorgeous Marcus was.

Instead, he sounded panicked as he exclaimed, "You need to get out of there, Romy! Right now. If the man in that photo is with you, play it cool. Just make some excuse, and as soon as you're out of the suite, fucking run."

"I don't understand. Why would I do that?"

"Because that man has been lying to you," Pete said. "His name's not Marcus. It's Mario Greco."

9

Marcus

When I returned to the suite, I hid the gift I'd bought for Romy under his pillow. It was just a silly little trinket—a snow globe, which made no sense for San Diego—but I thought he'd like it.

Then I went to join him on the patio, but he wasn't there. I went back inside and called his name, but there was nothing but silence.

A minute later, my phone beeped. I smiled when I saw the text was from Romy. Then I read it, and my gut seized up.

It said: *Please tell me you're not Mario Greco. Please, Marcus, don't be him. It's going to fucking break me if it turns out you've been lying to me this whole time.*

I whispered, "Oh god, this can't be happening," as I called Romy's number. When he answered, I blurted, "Baby, where are you?"

"That doesn't matter. I just need to know, are you Mario Greco?"

"Please, come back. Let's talk about this."

"Just tell me if it's true. I need to know." His voice was shaky.

I pressed my eyes shut and asked, "How did you find out?"

Silence.

After a few moments, I asked, "Baby, are you still there?"

Finally, he said, "So, it's true. You're the sociopath who terrorized my family."

I sat down on the floor and clutched the phone. "I need you to know I never ordered my men to kidnap your brother or smash up your mom's bar. They came up with that shit on their own when I was in New York, and when I found out, I fired my entire crew."

"Why should I believe that? Why should I believe a single thing you say?"

"It's the truth," I said softly.

"Did you know my brother's fiancé got shot during that kidnapping?"

"Shit. No, I didn't. Is he okay?"

"Yeah, but that's not the point. He could have been killed! My brother could have, too, since your men decided to shoot their way through a plate glass window to get to him."

I whispered, "I didn't want any of that to happen."

"Was I just part of some plan? Did you think you could hurt my brother by...by seducing me? By making me fall for you?"

"No! Romy, you have to believe me. There was no plan."

"Why'd you come to the bar that night? It was after hours, so no one should have been there. Did you plan to finish what you started and smash it up again? Or maybe burn it down? That'd really show my brother, right?" The anger in his voice kept building.

"No! I didn't go there to do anything like that. Like I said, I never intended to target the bar in the first place."

"Bullshit, Marcus! Or Mario. Whatever your name is. You didn't just randomly decide to visit the bar at three a.m."

"It's Marcus. I didn't lie about that, or about anything else. I just omitted some information." That sounded pathetic, and I knew it.

"That was a pretty fucking important piece of information!"

"I know, and I'm so sorry, baby."

"Stop calling me that, and tell me why you came to the bar that night!"

"I guess I went to the bar on the off chance I'd find your brother there. I wanted to pick a fight. But I found you instead, and you were sweet, and beautiful, and in pain, and I just…I wanted to help you."

"I don't believe you." His voice was quiet now. I could hear the pain in it.

"It's true, I swear. You were never part of any plan. You were just…a beautiful miracle."

"Please stop trying to manipulate me. Haven't you done enough?"

"Romy, please come back and talk to me. Let me explain."

"No. I can't tell the truth from your lies, and seeing you…seeing you might put me back under your spell."

"If you won't come here, then I'll come to you. Please—"

"You really shouldn't do that," he said. "My brother will want to shoot you when he finds out about this, and I really don't want him to go to jail for murder."

"Romy—"

"Don't bother trying to call me. I'm blocking your number." His voice was so quiet when he said, "Goodbye, Marcus."

The phone went dead. I stared at it for a long time, as if he might possibly call back.

But that was all he'd wanted to say to me.

After a while—minutes or hours, I couldn't be sure—I got up and looked around. I felt dazed. Hollow.

Then I went to my suite and started to pack.

I'd fucked up, big time, but I wasn't going to let it end like that. I couldn't. Romy meant way too much to me to just give up without trying to talk to him face-to-face. He'd be able to look me in the eye and see I was telling the truth, and that would make all the difference.

At least, I hoped so.

And yeah, it really might get me shot, because it sounded like he was going straight to his well-armed big brother. But that was just a chance I had to take.

10

Romy

After I spoke to Pete, who swore to me repeatedly that really was Mario Greco in the photo, I ran around the suite and shoved my stuff into my luggage in about ninety seconds flat. My heart was racing as I snuck out of the hotel like a spy, taking an indirect route because I really wanted to avoid Marcus.

Part of me didn't believe he was Greco. He couldn't be! But I was so rattled and confused that I just couldn't face him.

I hopped into a cab and asked the driver to take me to the airport, and after a few minutes, I sent Marcus a text. I should have known he'd call right back. The conversation that followed left me feeling totally wrung out. The cab driver kept checking on me in the mirror every few seconds, because I almost melted down in her back seat.

Once my hands stopped shaking, I sent Pete a text letting him know I'd made it out of the hotel without incident. He called me right back, and after we dissected the conversation I'd had with Marcus, he said, "I'm glad you're okay, and that you're coming home."

"Actually, I'm going to San Francisco, because I need to talk to my brother. I figured it would be best to do that face-to-face, but I'm dreading it."

"Why?"

"Because he's going to go on a rampage," I said. "As soon as I tell him what happened, he'll gather an army and go after him with everything he's got. At the same time, Marcus has the resources to build an army of his own, and he and my brother will probably wage an all-out war. People could die, Pete, because I was stupid and too trusting."

"So, are you sure you should tell him?"

"This affects him, so I can't keep it a secret. If this was all some sort of scheme to get to my brother through me…" I thought about that and shook my head. "It doesn't make sense, though. If he just wanted to find Adriano or cause him harm, there are much quicker and more efficient ways to go about that, besides seducing me. So, what was he playing at?"

"Maybe nothing," Pete said. "Maybe it wasn't some grand scheme to use you to get to your brother. He could have been telling the truth about just randomly finding you at the bar. Hell, he even could have been sincere about falling for you. But that doesn't change the fact that he was lying, *that whole time.* He let you get close to him, while purposely withholding the fact that he's your brother's worst enemy. You know what Mario Greco did to your family, and what he's capable of."

"But he seemed so sweet and genuine…"

"It's actually terrifying that he could put on another persona like that," Pete said. "Talk about a wolf in sheep's clothing."

"How could I be that wrong about someone? I feel like I can't trust my instincts anymore, because I didn't pick up on a single red flag."

"Don't blame yourself, Romy. You're an open, trusting person. It's your nature."

I muttered, "Which is a nice way of saying I'm naïve and clueless."

"Please don't do that. Don't blame yourself, or beat yourself up.

You're the victim here, and that man was obviously a master manipulator."

"Yeah. Look, I'd better go. I need to get online and find a flight to San Francisco. But thank you, Pete, for everything. You're a good friend."

After I promised to check in soon, I ended the call and pulled up an airline's website. I couldn't read it though, because tears were blurring my vision.

I refused to break down and cry, though. Instead, I dragged a hand over my eyes and took a deep breath. Then I tapped into the thing that was fueling me and keeping me moving forward, instead of totally falling apart—pure, undiluted anger.

I had almost no memory of the airport in San Diego, or the steps I'd taken to buy a ticket and get myself onto a plane. The flight was a blur, too. So, when I stepped out of the terminal in San Francisco, it felt like waking up from a hazy dream.

I blinked a few times and looked around as I hugged my bags to my chest. Everyone around me seemed to be in a huge hurry, and the busy loading zone up ahead with all those cars coming and going was complete madness.

After a minute, I spotted my brother's fiancé hurrying toward me. Jack was flawless as ever, from his stylish sandy blond hair and a neatly trimmed beard to his expensive blue suit. I dropped my bags a second before he grabbed me in a hug. Then he looked me over and asked, "Are you okay? Your message about needing to talk to Reno had us both worried."

"No, I'm really not."

"What happened?"

"Way too much to discuss here."

We both practically had to yell because it was so loud, between the car engines, the noisy swarms of people, and the honking horns. There was also a frazzled traffic cop relentlessly blowing a whistle.

He was trying to stop people from parking in the loading zone, and he'd just set his sights on my brother's big, black SUV.

Adriano had decided to momentarily abandon the vehicle, so he could come and fetch Jack and me. He was so tall that it was easy to spot him weaving through the crowd. Needless to say, he looked annoyed, because all this chaos was grating on his nerves.

When he reached my side, he said, "Hiya, kid." Then he shoved his dark hair off his forehead and grabbed my bags. Like his fiancé, he was overdressed in a nice suit, though his was charcoal gray. There was a frown line between his thick, dark brows, and he tried to shepherd both of us toward the SUV as he said, "Can we get moving please, before that low budget rent-a-cop slaps a ticket on my windshield?"

As we made our way to the curb, I almost got run over by a tiny woman with a rolling cart heaped with luggage. Eventually, we reached the Land Rover. Adriano chucked my bags in the back while Jack and I both stood there and insisted the other take the passenger seat. I relented when my brother yelled, "I love you both, but I swear to god I'm leaving your asses here if you don't get in this fucking SUV!"

The moment we were all seated, I grabbed for my seat belt, because I knew what was coming next. And there it was. He saw an opening and shot from the curb, like some sort of deranged Indy car driver who was determined to overtake the pack. As he wove through several lanes of traffic, Jack muttered, "Jesus, Mary, and Joseph."

I didn't think he was actually religious, but my brother's aggressive way of dealing with traffic could make anyone toss up a prayer, just in case they were about to meet their maker. Fortunately, we made it out of the airport and back to San Francisco in one piece.

For the past couple of months, Adriano and Jack had been splitting their time between San Francisco and their home in Vegas. It gave them a chance to get to know Adriano's family on his dad's side, who they'd only recently met. I could see them putting down roots here at some point, but for now they were renting one of those places meant for executives on extended business trips—a furnished townhouse that felt a bit like a hotel.

I was grateful for its guest room. It was small, beige-on-beige, and pretty generic like the rest of the place, but it was also cozy and private. After I dropped my stuff onto the bed, used the restroom, and washed up, I paused and scrubbed my hands over my face.

This was going to suck. The fact that Adriano would be furious with Marcus was a given. But on top of that, he'd probably start questioning my judgement. It had always been an uphill battle to get him to think of me as an adult. Hell, he even called me "kid," and this was going to be a major setback. It would also probably kick his overprotectiveness into hyperdrive. I couldn't put it off though, so I left the bedroom and went to find him.

He and Jack were sitting close together on the living room couch, having a hushed conversation. Before they realized I was in the room, Jack caressed my brother's cheek and kissed him gently. Normally, that beautiful, all-consuming love between the two of them made me happy. Right now though, it made me feel lonely.

They moved apart—just a little—when they realized I was standing there. I took a seat on a club chair on the other side of the coffee table and cleared my throat before saying, "This is really hard for me, so please, let me get all of it out before you say anything or start asking questions."

I then proceeded to tell them the whole story, from how I'd met Marcus to the call from Pete this afternoon and everything in between—aside from the sex, obviously. They could figure that out without my help.

Adriano went very still, and when I finished talking he didn't say anything at first. That was totally out of character for him. He should have been pacing and ranting. Somehow, the stillness was a lot more unnerving.

Jack was clearly worried about it, too. He rested his hand on his fiancé's arm, which reminded me of holding down the lever on a hand grenade to keep it from exploding.

When he finally spoke, my brother said, in a low voice, "Show me the picture, the one where Pete said he recognized Greco."

I pulled it up on my phone and leaned across the coffee table to hand it over. I ended up passing it to him face-down, and he gritted his teeth when he turned it over. I asked, "Is that him? Is it Mario Greco?" I already knew the answer, but I was hoping for a miracle.

He gave a single nod, and then he carefully placed my phone on the coffee table. A muscle was working in his jaw, but other than that, he remained unnaturally still for another minute.

Finally, he said, in a voice so calm it was eerie, "I'm going to kill him."

My brother stood up and started to leave the room, and his fiancé called after him, "Where are you going?"

"To make a phone call."

Jack turned to me with worry in his eyes. "This is bad. He's probably calling his dad's relatives. We both know they're ex-mafia, and they're not going to try to talk him out of going after Greco. Just the opposite."

"I know, and I'm going to talk to him when he—well, not calms down. He's too calm right now, and it's freaking me out. But I'm going to talk to him when he's a little more rational. The good news is, he'll never find Marcus. He doesn't even have a permanent address right now. And if he can't find him, we don't have to worry about either of them getting shot."

Jack studied me closely as he said, "You still care about that guy, don't you?"

I nodded. "I can't just shut it off. We had this intense connection, and…how could I be so wrong about someone? He seemed kind, and gentle. But he might be responsible for some truly terrible things, so how do I reconcile that? It would have to be the most extreme case of Jekyll and Hyde anyone's ever seen."

"*Might* be responsible?"

"When I talked to him on my way to the airport, he said his crew took it upon themselves to wreck the bar and abduct Reno. Apparently, Marcus was out of town at the time, and they never cleared it with him. He also said he fired all of them for what they'd done. I really need that to be true. It's one thing to know he's a liar, but if he was actually responsible for terrorizing my family, it's so much worse. It means I failed to recognize a monster when it was staring me in the face."

"But who knows what's true and what isn't at this point?"

"Not me, obviously." I rubbed my forehead, as if that might actually ease the headache that was brewing, and muttered, "It's too much to make sense of right now. I just want to take a very long, very hot shower and climb into bed for a week or two. But first, I need to talk my brother down from his murderous rampage…"

We both got up, and Jack said, "I'll talk to him. He won't be able to do anything tonight anyway, because like you said, he'll have no idea where to find Greco. Go take that shower and get some rest. You've been through hell today, so taking care of yourself needs to be your main priority."

I looked down at myself, only then realizing I'd come all this way in Hawaiian print swim trunks, flip flops, and an oversized hoodie. "All I have with me is dirty laundry."

"I'll leave some clothes on your bed while you're in the shower."

"Thank you, Jack." I gave him a hug and told him, "I'm sorry about showing up out of the blue and disrupting your lives like this."

"Don't you dare feel guilty about coming here! You're exactly where you belong—with your family." He let go of me and gave me a light, playful shove. "Now go and stay in the shower until you've used up every last drop of hot water. I expect to see some major self-care happening. Otherwise, there *will* be nagging and lectures."

"Alright, I'm going." I started to leave the room, but then I turned back to him and admitted, "I was really falling for him, Jack. I thought it was mutual, and now I'm just so confused. Was it all a lie?"

There was so much sympathy in his eyes when he whispered, "I wish I knew."

11

Marcus

Shortly before midnight, I stepped out onto the hotel balcony and shivered. No wonder, since I was still dressed in the T-shirt and shorts I'd put on that morning in San Diego.

That felt like a million years ago. So much had happened since then, and a lot of it was a blur. I had only the vaguest recollection of packing my things, checking out of the resort, and getting myself to the airport. I didn't remember where I'd left the Porsche, either. Wherever it was, maybe someone would call it in, and the rental agency would send someone to pick it up. If not, I really didn't give a fuck.

I braced my hands on the cold steel railing and looked around me. My suite was on the top floor of the hotel. From here, San Francisco sprawled in every direction, blanketed in a million lights.

Romy was out there somewhere—in a room with one of those lights, or maybe in the darkness in between. He'd mentioned his brother, so I was sure he'd come here instead of returning to Las Vegas. And of course I'd followed him, because I desperately needed to talk to him, apologize, and beg him to take me back.

I just had no idea how I was going to find him.

12

Romy

After about a week spent moping around their house, Reno and Jack convinced me to go with them to Sunday dinner at their friends' house. I didn't really want to go anywhere, but everyone was starting to worry about me, so I scraped myself up and went along to try to make them think I was okay. In reality, I was a mess, and I didn't see that changing any time soon.

It was a five-minute walk to our destination, and Pete texted along the way to see how I was doing. He'd been great about checking in regularly. I told him I was fine, because I didn't want him to worry, and when I asked how he was, he sent back a smiley face emoji. Then he wrote: *I've started dating one of the big, hot muscle daddies your brother hired to guard the bar. His name is Guillermo, and it was lust at first sight.*

I wrote: *I'm happy for you. I didn't realize Reno had hired guards.*

Pete's next message said: *Oh yeah, there are teams of two here on eight-hour shifts, literally 24/7. I'm surprised Adriano didn't tell you.*

So was I. After we exchanged a couple more texts, I glanced at my brother. He was holding Jack's hand, and each of them was carrying a bottle of wine, as their contribution to this dinner we were attending. They'd both tried to dress down, which meant they were in nice jeans and button-down shirts with the sleeves rolled back. I wondered if they'd planned to coordinate their outfits like that.

As I returned the phone to my pocket, I said, "That was Pete. What's this about a round-the-clock security detail at Mom's bar?"

"It's just a precaution," he told me with a shrug.

"Because of Marcus?"

"We don't really know why he came to the bar the night you met him, and I figured there was no harm in upping security." It seemed like overkill, but I didn't feel like arguing.

I was pleasantly surprised when our destination turned out to be a funky pink Victorian with rainbow curtains in every window and a big Pride flag above the front porch. Just as surprising was the eclectic group of people who lived there. I'd expected buttoned down guys in suits, like Jack and Reno. Instead, the place had a bohemian vibe, and just about the entire rainbow flag was represented among its many residents and their dinner guests.

Soon after we arrived, Jack made a point of introducing me to Timothy, a gorgeous blue-eyed brunet with unruly curls and a slim build. Then he made an excuse and left us alone together. Was it my imagination, or was he trying to set us up?

Timothy turned to me and said, "I heard you recently had a bad breakup. Are you doing okay?"

"No, but let's pretend I said yes so I don't drag the mood down. When did Jack tell you?"

"Technically, he was telling his good friend JoJo, not me, when he came over for tea a couple of days ago. She's that pretty blonde bombshell across the room, in case you haven't been introduced yet. Anyway, I'm super nosy, so I butted into their conversation. I missed most of the details, but it sounded messy."

"You could say that."

"Been there." Timothy slumped dramatically. Then he perked up and pushed a dark curl out of his eyes. "You know what we need? A huge batch of gin and tonics, to drown your sorrows. Let's go make some."

With that, he started weaving through the crowded living room, and I tried to keep up. Once we reached the cheerful pink and purple kitchen at the back of the house, he began to gather ingredients, and I said, "This place is amazing. How long have you lived here?"

"About a month. One of my friend Noah's boyfriends used to rent my room, so it became available when they all moved in together around the holidays."

I repeated, "One of his boyfriends?"

He nodded as he poured a hell of a lot of gin into a pitcher. "He's part of a throuple with two guys named Kel and Hudson. They're very cute together."

"That's awesome."

"So, Jack said you're here visiting from Vegas. Will you be staying in San Francisco for a while?"

"I don't know. I'm on an open-ended leave of absence from work, but there's literally no plan."

"Well, if you decide to stay here long-term and need a job, the restaurant where I work is always looking for servers. Everyone thinks the owner is a jerk, so they keep quitting. And he is, but like, once you accept that, it's a pretty okay place to work."

"That's good to know." Fortunately, I had enough savings to live on for at least three months, so there wasn't an immediate need to bring in a paycheck.

When my phone buzzed, I said, "Excuse me for a minute," and pulled it from the pocket of my hoodie. It turned out to be a message from my mom, which read: *Just wanted you to know I'm thinking about you, sweetie. Call if you need anything.*

The day after I'd arrived in San Francisco, I'd finally had a very long and overdue video call with her. We talked about my dad, and then I told her about Marcus and how he'd turned out to be Mario Greco, and it was hard to say which one upset her more. Since then, she'd been checking on me every day.

I sent a reply letting her know I was having dinner with Jack and Reno at the home of some of their friends, and she wrote: *Thank god you've finally left the house! Your brother said you've been moping, and that's not good for you. Go have fun and I'll talk to you soon.*

I hated the fact that my mom and brother were worried about me. I'd have to start leaving the house more often to make them think I was okay, not that I was up for much. But maybe I could start reading at a café instead of in my room or something.

While I'd been texting, Timothy finished making the cocktails. He filled two mason jars and handed me one as he said, "So, tell me, Romy. What do you do for fun?"

"I read a lot, and I watch movies." I probably should have dressed that up a bit, but there it was.

"Well, if you decide you want to go out and meet someone new, I can be your night club tour guide. I honestly believe the best way to get over someone is to get under someone else."

There was no way I was ready for that, but I told him it sounded great, just so I didn't come across as a total hermit. Then I asked, "What else are you into, besides the local club scene?"

"I love skateboarding, roller blading, mountain biking—basically, if it's physical, I'm into it. Last week, I started learning how to pole dance. That's been super fun."

I took a sip of my extremely boozy gin and tonic before saying, "That sounds cool. I watched a video of a men's pole dancing competition once, and it all looked so athletic and graceful."

"Would you want to try it?"

"Me?"

"Sure, why not?"

I frowned and told him, "I'm not exactly coordinated."

"That doesn't matter. I go to this great, super inclusive studio, and there are people from all walks of life and every skill level. Come with me and try it out! The first class is free, so what do you have to lose?"

"I can't even sort of imagine myself pole dancing, and that's actually why I'm going to say yes to this. I've been thinking I really need to try new things, so it's worth a shot, right?" It would also get me out of the house, so my family could quit worrying about me.

Timothy's blue eyes lit up, and he exclaimed, "Absolutely! My class is Tuesdays and Thursdays at ten a.m. I work the dinner shift, so my days are wide open."

"Text me the address, and I'll be there this Tuesday."

We exchanged numbers, and he beamed at me and said, "You're going to love it. The studio is owned by the most drop-dead gorgeous guy named Dare. Sadly, he's married, but I still appreciate the eye candy."

Just then, a group of people came into the kitchen. Timothy squealed and grabbed a tall brunet in a hug before introducing me to Noah and his boyfriends.

Then a couple named Lark and Dylan came in, who I'd met when we first arrived. They pulled two enormous pans of lasagna out of the oven and put in four cookie sheets lined with garlic bread as Lark announced, "Dinner's in ten minutes! We've set the tables in the backyard since we're such a big group tonight, but it's a little chilly. Grab a throw blanket or an extra jacket on your way outside. You'll find both stacked beside the back door."

I expected Timothy to forget about me now that his friends were here. Instead, he linked his arm with mine and said, "Let's hurry, before all the cute coats are gone. I don't feel like going all the way upstairs for one of mine, and some of the loaners are a crime against fashion."

In all, there were twenty-one people at dinner. In addition to the seven who lived there, most of the others were former residents of the pink Victorian. Apparently this was a weekly thing with a core group who always attended, and others who came as often as they could.

The food was great, and I enjoyed the company and the conversation. But after we ate, I pulled Jack and Reno aside and told them I was headed home. My brother immediately looked concerned and asked, "Are you alright, kid?"

I assured him I was fine, but he still offered to go back to the townhouse with me. "Actually, I could use a little time to myself," I admitted. "It's been a while since I've been around so many people, and my social batteries are nearly empty."

He was too much of an extrovert to get it, but Jack did. He gave me his key and said, "We'll be home in about an hour. This usually doesn't run very late."

"Is it alright if I use your bathroom while you're gone? I could really go for a long, hot bath." I was freezing, and the townhouse's smaller downstairs bathroom didn't have a tub.

"Of course," Jack said. "Help yourself to my bubble bath, too. I just bought a good one that'll make your skin feel fabulous. It's supposed to smell like mango and passionfruit though, but really it just smells like strawberries."

I thanked him and went to say goodbye to Timothy, who made me promise to show up at that class on Tuesday. Then I thanked my hostesses before cutting through the house and heading out the front door.

It had gotten dark during dinner, and the breeze had picked up. I wrapped my arms around myself as I hurried up the hill.

Once I got to the townhouse, I went straight upstairs. Most of the top floor consisted of a spacious main bedroom and its adjoining bathroom, which were by far the nicest rooms in this place.

On accident, I poured in too much bubble bath as the tub filled. A thick mass of white bubbles formed as I quickly stripped down. Jack was right, it smelled like strawberries, despite what the label claimed.

It felt wonderful when I lowered myself into the water, which was right on the verge of being too hot. I leaned back, exhaled slowly, and closed my eyes. That moment of peace was short-lived though, because my thoughts immediately drifted to Marcus.

I sighed and sunk lower into the bubbles.

It was an ongoing struggle not to think about him constantly. I tried to keep myself distracted, but as soon as I let my guard down, there he was. I'd replayed every day we'd spent together over and over, dissecting everything he'd said and done, and I was still trying to make sense of it all. Now here I was, climbing back on that same treadmill.

I ended up staying in the bath and mentally going around in

circles until the water cooled. Eventually, I realized my brother and his fiancé would be home soon, so I climbed out of the tub and pulled the plug on the drain. After I dried off, I wrapped a towel around my hips and gathered my clothes and shoes into a bundle before leaving the bathroom.

In the main bedroom, a chair and side table were positioned beside a pair of French doors leading to a balcony. Someone had left a mug there, on top of a stack of books, so I decided to be helpful and take it to the kitchen. But when I went to retrieve it, I got distracted by one of the books and began reading the blurb on the back cover.

An odd sound caught my attention, and I looked up from the book and tried to figure out what I'd heard. When it happened again, I realized something had bounced off the glass doors. I put my things on the chair and went out onto the narrow balcony to investigate.

I stepped on a small, smooth pebble and kicked it aside. Then I leaned over the railing and looked around. The closest streetlight was out, so it was darker than it should have been.

Something moved in the shadows. My breath caught as Marcus stepped into the light spilling from the townhouse's windows and said, "I really need to talk to you, Romy."

13

Marcus

I wasn't sure I had the right house, not until I caught a glimpse of Romy through a pair of French doors on the second floor. Going up and ringing the doorbell wasn't an option, since I had no idea if his brother was home, and getting shot really wasn't on my to-do list. Instead, I found a few pebbles in the landscaping and went old school by tossing them at the glass doors.

Fortunately, he heard them and came out onto the balcony to investigate. He wore nothing but a towel around his slender hips, and he was achingly beautiful. I was so captivated that for a moment, all I could do was stare.

My pulse was racing, and I drew a ragged breath as I stepped forward, into the light. I was so nervous that I could barely speak. Finally, I managed, "I really need to talk to you, Romy."

He went completely still. Was he afraid of me? That would break my heart.

But once the initial shock wore off, he exclaimed, "You can't be here, Marcus!"

"Please, just hear me out."

"Listen to me! My brother is going to come home any minute. If he finds you here, you're dead!"

"Just give me five minutes. That's all I ask."

"You need to go!"

"I'm begging you. Please, Romy. I have to apologize and try to explain."

He seemed almost panicked as he shifted his gaze to the street and blurted, "Fine, but not here."

"Okay. Tell me when and where, and I'll be there."

"I don't know. I'm not very familiar with San Francisco."

"How about my hotel?"

"No. I want to meet in public." That stung, but I deserved it after breaking his trust. "It just has to be someplace where there's no chance of running into my brother, his relatives, or any of the people he's hired to find you."

"I'll meet you anywhere you want."

He pushed his hair off his forehead and thought about it for a moment before saying,

"There's a red and green Chinese pavilion on a lake in Golden Gate Park. I saw it on a post card once. Meet me there tomorrow at ten a.m."

"I'll be there."

"Now please get out of here, Marcus. And don't go that way, or you're going to run into Adriano." He pointed to the right.

"Okay. I'll see you tomorrow."

I hurried away, but I didn't go far. My rental car was parked two houses down. After I took a seat behind the wheel, curiosity compelled me to wait and see what would happen.

Romy had been telling the truth, and no wonder he'd seemed frantic. Not two minutes later, his brother came around the corner. He was on foot and holding hands with a man who made him look huge by comparison.

The sight of Adriano Dombruso made me bristle. I'd hated him from the moment we'd met. I doubted he remembered it, but I couldn't forget. An associate had brought me to Dombruso's underground gambling club. I'd only been out of prison for about six months, and I was far from polished—I knew that. I'd had long hair and a thick beard, and I'd probably been wearing jeans and leather, because that was what I lived in back then.

Dombruso had taken one look at me and denied me access to his club. Apparently I wasn't good enough to hang out with the criminals and lowlifes who frequented his establishment. I had a very short fuse back then, so of course I got in his face and tried to start a fight. I'd never forget his smug grin when four of his men grabbed me and dragged me away from him—because of course, he was too good to fight me himself.

He went back inside as punches started flying. Since it was four against one, those men ended up beating the shit out of me. It wasn't just humiliating. The contact I'd spent weeks trying to befriend wanted nothing to do with me after that. I had to go back to Art and tell him how I'd screwed up that important connection, and he was so disappointed in me. I fucking hated letting him down.

And needless to say, Dombruso made himself an enemy that day.

When I came back to Vegas years later using the alias Mario Greco, I was a different man. I'd learned how to play the game with bespoke suits, expensive haircuts, and watches that cost as much as a car—all the outward signs of success and power.

I was on a mission—to honor Art's wishes by making a mark in Vegas. The way I chose to accomplish that goal was by building an illegal gambling empire, the likes of which Sin City had never seen before. It turned out one of the minor players standing in my way was Adriano Dombruso. That gave me an excuse to make his life hell.

Seeing him tonight, all those memories came flooding back. I still hated him, but I had to push it aside, for Romy's sake.

Dombruso and his companion climbed the stairs to the front door, and then they paused and shared a lingering kiss. Great, now I felt like a peeping Tom.

I waited until they went inside before starting the engine, because I didn't want to attract their attention. Then I drove back to my hotel and immediately did an internet search for pavilions in

Golden Gate Park. It was a relief when I found what had to be the right one.

A glance at my watch told me I had almost twelve hours to kill until I got to see Romy again. It was going to be a long night.

14

Romy

My heart was pounding as I closed the French doors. How on earth had Marcus found this place? And what would have happened if my brother had come home just then?

I grabbed my clothes and shoes from the chair and hurried downstairs. When I reached my room, I shut the door behind me, threw on a T-shirt and pajama pants, and climbed into bed.

Not ten seconds later, I heard my brother and Jack come home. Damn, that was a close call.

When one of them knocked on my door, it made me jump. In an attempt to look casual, I snatched a paperback from the night-stand, opened it to a random page, and called, "Come in!" Fortunately, I noticed the book was upside down and corrected it as the door swung open.

Jack smiled at me and said, "I saw your light was on, so I thought I'd check and see if you wanted some tea. I'm about to make myself some."

"No, thanks."

He tilted his head as he asked, "Are you okay? You're pretty flushed."

"Yeah, fine. The bath was really hot." Technically, I wasn't lying to him, though the color in my cheeks was probably because I was freaking the hell out.

Jack gestured at the book in my hands and asked, "Are you enjoying that so far? It's one of my favorites."

I nodded. I'd actually only borrowed it from him that morning and hadn't started it yet. But it was open to the middle of the book, so I had to pretend.

"I'll let you get back to it. Good night, Romy. See you in the morning."

"Good night."

As soon as he was gone, I returned the book to the nightstand and slumped against the pillows. I felt like an ass for that little charade, but I couldn't tell him I was freaking out because I'd just seen Marcus. If I did that, he'd tell my brother, and the massive manhunt that was currently happening in Las Vegas would shift to San Francisco.

How the hell had Marcus pulled that off?

There should have been no way for him to find this place. My brother had rented it under the name of a fictitious business, just like he did with everything. When you made your living illegally, it was important to hide both your whereabouts and your finances from rivals, the IRS, law enforcement, and so on. Marcus obviously did the same thing, otherwise Adriano's people would have tracked him down by now.

But if Marcus could find my (and by default, Adriano's) secret location, couldn't my brother do the same thing in reverse? I hadn't been all that worried about the fact that he was searching for Marcus, because I'd assumed finding him would be impossible. Maybe I'd been overconfident about that.

Wait—was my brother in danger, now that Marcus knew where to find him?

When I'd seen him in front of the house, all I could think about was Marcus's safety, not the other way around. Why was that?

After I thought about it, some things came into focus.

Adriano was fiercely protective of my mom and me. I'd always known that. I didn't believe he had it in him to kill anyone...but if he thought that was the only way to keep his family safe, maybe he was capable of turning his back while one of his ex-mafia relatives did the job.

At the same time, no matter who he was or what he'd done in the past, I realized I really did believe Marcus cared about me and wouldn't want to hurt me—not after what we'd shared. I felt it in my gut. That also meant he wouldn't harm my brother, because he knew how much Adriano meant to me.

And yes, I cared about Marcus, too. But that didn't necessarily mean I'd be able to forgive him.

I had a million questions and a lot I needed to say to him, and I was glad we'd have a chance to talk. So much was hanging on that conversation. It was going to reveal whether there was even the slightest chance of working things out, or if everything we'd started to build was lost forever.

15

Marcus

I was more than an hour early for my meeting with Romy, since I'd been worried about finding the pavilion in such a massive park. I'd read it was on a manmade lake though, and that turned out to be easy enough to find.

The lake's parking lot was adjacent to a boat house that rented paddle boats and canoes by the hour. It was probably vibrant and bustling in the summer, but on this foggy Monday morning in early February, it was empty and a bit depressing.

After I pocketed my keys, I started walking. Eventually, I rounded a bend and my destination came into view. It was actually really striking, with its red supports and jade green tile roof.

I crossed a bridge leading to an island in the middle of the lake, and then I went inside the pavilion to get a closer look. It was basically an ornate, open-air gazebo in a Chinese architectural style. There was a built-in table and stools in the center of it, with benches around the inside perimeter. I took a seat on a bench, but after just a few seconds, I got up and started pacing.

I was worried about how Romy would feel about this location. He'd wanted to meet in public, but this barely qualified. Would it make him uncomfortable to be alone with me like this, after I'd shattered his trust? Maybe the best thing to do would be to go back and meet him at the boat house. It was closed and no one was there either, but it didn't feel as isolated as this did.

Just as I started to leave, I spotted him coming up the path to the pavilion. He was almost as early as I was.

"I know this probably isn't what you had in mind," I said, as I gestured at our surroundings. "So, if you'd rather meet somewhere else—"

"It's fine."

He wasn't afraid of me. Thank god. Anything else I could work with, but that...that would have been devastating.

Romy strode past me into the pavilion, took a seat on the stone table, and rested his feet on one of the stools. Since he was facing the open doorway, there was no place for me to sit—not without making him pivot around to face me. It was a total power move on his part, and I had mad respect for it.

He pinned me with a sharp stare and said, "Tell me you didn't kidnap my brother or wreck my mom's bar. I know what you said on the phone, but I need you to look me in the eye and swear your men weren't carrying out your orders."

I held his gaze steadily. "I swear on my life I didn't know they were going to do either of those things. I was furious when I found out, and I fired every last one of them." I took a breath and made myself add, "I'm still responsible, though."

"In what way?"

"I'm the one who declared war on your brother in the first place. If my troops ran amok when my back was turned, it's still on me. It shows I wasn't strong enough as a leader, and I failed to keep them in line. They should have been so afraid of me that they didn't even take a shit without asking permission."

"It makes a huge difference to me, though. I didn't understand how you could do either of those things, and it turns out you didn't. It's going to make a difference to Adriano, too, and—"

"No, it won't. Like me, he'll understand that what was done in my name is my responsibility."

Romy watched me for a few moments before asking, "Should I call you Marcus or Mario?"

"My real name is Marcus Greene. The other is one of several aliases I've used over the years. For the record, I had every intention of telling you about Mario Greco. I was just waiting for the right time."

"The right time? You had an entire week!"

"I know, but I didn't want to tell you while we were in San Diego."

His voice rose. "When *did* you plan to tell me, on our five-year wedding anniversary?"

That took both of us by surprise. He obviously hadn't meant to paint a picture of our happily ever after, but there it was.

"I guess I was going to tell you when we got back to Las Vegas, not that I had any of this planned out," I said. "That was true right from the start. I never planned on meeting you that night at your mom's bar, and I sure as hell never planned on being wildly attracted to you. When I agreed to go to the coast, I was picturing a couple of days fucking each other's brains out in a hotel room before going our separate ways."

"But that's not what happened."

"No, it isn't. Not at all. Instead, for the very first time in my life, I developed real feelings for someone. It took me totally by surprise. I didn't think I was capable of it, which is why I never imagined there'd be any harm in going away with you.

"But then every day—hell, every hour—that passed, you and I grew closer, and it got harder and harder to tell you I was Mario Greco. That week with you felt like...like stepping into another world, or into someone else's life.

"I was feeling and experiencing things I never even dared to hope for, things I never believed I could have, and I didn't want it to end. But I knew it would, the second I told you the truth.

"I swear to god, Romy, I didn't want to deceive you, but I knew the truth would ruin everything. It would drive you away, and I couldn't stand the thought of that. I know it's selfish, and I know I'm a terrible person. I *know* that. I've always known it."

I dropped to my knees as my voice broke, and I stared at the floor as the words just kept spilling out of me. "I fucked up, and I hurt you, and maybe that was inevitable. Maybe I can't be anything but a monster. I really am so sorry, but it's not enough. I know that too, and I don't blame you for hating me. I don't deserve you. I never did. You were always way too good for me."

Romy muttered, "Damn it, Marcus," and climbed off the table. Then he came over to me, and I leaned into him and buried my face in the soft fabric of his hoodie.

He began to stroke my hair, and after a while he said, "I would have done the same thing. If that was my secret, I wouldn't have known how to tell you, and I would have held back.

"But just because I understand it doesn't mean I instantly forgive you. It's going to take time to rebuild trust and get us back to where we were." I looked up at him and nodded, because I didn't trust my voice to work without cracking. He touched my cheek, so gently that it made my heart ache, and said, "Come on, let's sit down. I have a lot of questions for you."

I got up and followed him to one of the benches. I desperately wanted to move closer and to take his hand, but I hadn't earned that right.

Romy looked out at the mist hanging over the tranquil water while he gathered his thoughts. Finally, he said, "Tell me how you found my brother's house."

"I knew you'd come to San Francisco, because you'd mentioned your brother. I followed you here and hired six local private investigators to find you. I pitted them against each other by offering a huge bonus to whoever got me your address first. Your brother's smart, though. He doesn't put anything under his name, including rental agreements. So, ultimately, what it came down to was dumb luck.

"Yesterday, one of the PIs happened to be driving up your street on the way to an appointment. That was when she noticed an SUV with Nevada plates. It matched the description I'd given her of a vehicle I'd seen your brother driving in Vegas, so she figured she'd check it out. She parked in front of the house, and within a few hours, she managed to snap a photo of your brother. As soon as she sent me the picture, I knew I'd found you.

"I went to the address she gave me, but I obviously couldn't just walk up to the door, since your brother is probably out for blood. While I was standing on the sidewalk trying to figure out how to approach you, I saw you in that upstairs window. You know the rest." I grinned a little and added, "The irony wasn't lost on me, by the way."

"What irony?"

"You know—the fact that your name is Romeo, and we had our own balcony scene."

He grinned too and said, "I didn't even think of that. Although in Romeo and Juliet, he's not the one on the balcony."

"Close enough."

After a pause, he asked, "Did you disable the streetlight in front of the house, so you could skulk around in the darkness?"

"The PI did that. She was planning on round-the-clock surveillance if necessary and didn't want to be spotted sitting in her car."

A few more moments ticked by. Then he met and held my gaze. "Now that you know where he lives, will you try to hurt my brother?"

"Absolutely not. It's no secret that I can't stand him, but you adore him, so he's off limits."

He nodded, as if that was the answer he'd been expecting. Then he asked, "Why do you hate him so much?"

I told him the story of that day more than five years ago at his brother's club. Even though it was humiliating, I didn't hold back any of the details. Then I said, "I fully understand my role in all of that, by the way. If I hadn't lost my temper, it wouldn't have escalated the way it did."

"I can't believe he treated you like that." This information had definitely rattled him. "That's not the Adriano I know."

"Your brother and I are pretty similar, as much as I hate to admit it. When he's in that world, he's playing a role. He has to be the tough guy, or else people won't respect him. When he's with you, he can be himself. It's the same with me."

"We need to arrange a meeting between the two of you," he said. "Don't you think it's time to call off your feud?"

"I already called it off, but I'm guessing your brother is beyond furious right now. I assume you told him everything."

"I had to. At first, I didn't know if you'd been using me to get to him."

"I wasn't! I swear."

"I know. I figured that out pretty quickly. But right after the truth came out, I was shocked and furious, and I didn't know what to think."

After yet another lull in the conversation, I asked him, "How'd you find out I was Greco?"

"I texted a photo of us to a friend of mine, someone who'd been there when my brother confronted you back in October. He recognized you right away."

"Oh."

Romy glanced at me and asked, "Is that why you asked me to keep our photos private, because you didn't want to be found out?" I nodded and hung my head in shame. After a beat, he continued, "Anyway, my brother is in full war mode now, so don't go back to Vegas. He and his half-brother Dante have a whole team of mercenaries looking for you, and this morning he mentioned they're not the only ones doing that. I guess their people ran into some men from New York who are also very eager to find you. Did you know about that?"

"I assume they're Art's former associates. Their timing sucks, too. I don't have a crew anymore, not that I ever really trusted them to have my back. So right now, it's just me against your brother, his mafia relatives, their crew of hired mercenaries, and an assortment of east coast criminals. I don't like my odds."

"What are you going to do?"

"I have no idea. Did you tell anyone I'm in San Francisco?"

"No. I hate lying to my brother, and I felt like a real jerk this morning when he asked where I was going and I had to make something up. But he can't find out you're here. It's already dangerous for you, because all his ex-mafia relatives live in this city. If he moves the manhunt to San Francisco, it's game over."

"I'm sorry to put you in a position where you have to keep secrets."

"Don't apologize," he said. "That's a choice I made, because I want to keep you safe. I take full responsibility for it. And speaking of your safety, maybe you should think about getting out of San Francisco until this blows over. Anyplace besides here or Vegas would be a smart choice."

"I can't do that."

"Why not?"

"Because you're here," I said quietly, "and I need to be wherever you are."

Romy glanced at me, and his expression softened. He looked away again before saying, "Well, maybe I could go with you, or something."

Even though I really believed he cared about my safety, he wasn't ready to run away with me. Not by a long shot. We needed to rebuild our relationship from the ground-up, and that was going to take time.

I let him off the hook by saying, "We can't do that. You're an angel for suggesting it, but I'm not going to take you away from your family or ask you to go on the run with me. We'll just figure out another solution, one that doesn't involve running away." As if it was that simple.

~

We talked for another two hours. A lot of that time was spent walking around the island in slow laps, when we both got cold from sitting still.

Gradually, the fog burned off, the sky turned blue, and people began to arrive at the lake. As we returned to the pavilion after another lap, Romy turned to me and said, "I guess I should go. My brother and his fiancé will wonder what happened to me."

"Want to meet again tomorrow? Same time and place?"

When he said, "I can't," my heart sank. But then he continued, "I'm taking a pole dancing class at ten, so maybe we can meet in the afternoon."

"Really? That doesn't seem like something you'd be into."

"I know, and I guess that's kind of the point. I've spent my whole life…staying in my lane, I guess. I go to the gym, go to work, hang out at the bar my mom's owned since before I was born, and watch the same movies over and over, because they're comfortable. That's pretty much it.

"And the thing is, I know better than anyone that life is short. It's also extremely unpredictable. I was reminded of that every week at my job, and then when my dad died, it felt like the universe was grabbing me by the shoulders and shaking me.

"I've had a lot of time to think lately, and what I've realized is that I need to stop coasting and start living, shaking things up, and taking chances." He looked up at me and continued, "If there's such a thing as fate, it would make me think you arrived in my life exactly when you were supposed to. During that week we spent together in San Diego, it was as if I finally woke up. I felt alive, instead of just going through the motions. I still carry the essence of that with me, and it's causing a ripple effect in the rest of my life, from quitting my job to trying new things that are totally outside my comfort zone."

"Really? You're quitting your job?"

He nodded. "Right now, I'm on an extended leave of absence. But I'm planning to call my supervisor and tell him I won't be returning."

"That's huge," I said. "What do you think you'll do instead?"

"I have no idea. All I know is, that job was never the right fit for me, no matter how much I wanted it to be. I just couldn't develop a thick enough skin and remain unaffected by the stuff I had to deal with on a daily basis.

"I also realized after talking to you about it that I was sticking with the job for other people. I wanted to make my brother and my mom proud, and that took priority over how it was making me feel. But I deserve to be happy."

"You absolutely do. For what it's worth, I'm really proud of you for making such a big change and taking care of yourself."

He grinned at me. Then, for a long moment we both just stood there, as if we weren't quite sure what to do next. Finally, he brought the conversation back around by asking, "Anyway, how does meeting here at one tomorrow sound?"

"That works for me, but the lake might be more crowded at that time of day. Should we be worried about someone discovering us here?"

Romy thought about that before saying, "We should be fine. I can't imagine my brother or any of his relatives coming here. Why would they? Their idea of an outing is dinner in a nice restaurant, not visiting a lake in the park."

"Okay. I'll see you tomorrow then."

"Are you heading back to the parking lot?"

"No, I think I'll stay here a little longer."

He gave me a quick hug before starting down the path, and I leaned against one of the pavilion's supports and watched him leave. That had gone so much better than I could have hoped for. I knew I had a long way to go to earn back his trust, but he was giving me a chance. That was all I needed.

After a while, I started making my way back to the parking lot. I had a full day to kill and absolutely no idea how to pass the time.

What had I done before I met Romy? Who had I been back then?

So much of my time had revolved around Art—trying to earn the respect of the closest thing to a father I'd ever had, and fulfilling my obligations to him, even after he died.

When was it enough?

Yes, he'd protected me, and he'd left me a literal fortune, but how much more of my life was I expected to give him in return? So far, it had been six years. Since they'd followed right on the heels of ten years in prison, that meant none of my adult life had been mine—except for these last two weeks with Romy, and then without him.

Now I needed to figure out how to put the past behind me once and for all. It was the only way Romy and I had any shot at a future together.

16

Romy

The next morning, I decided to try to have a conversation with my brother. We'd just finished breakfast, and he and I were lingering over coffee while Jack was upstairs taking a shower.

I retrieved the coffee pot and refilled our mugs before asking, "Can we talk?"

"Yeah, of course."

I took a breath and said, "I need you to call off your manhunt. This is between Marcus and me, but you're using what happened between us to fuel your own vendetta."

He met my gaze and asked, "Did you hear from him?"

I hated lying to his face, so I tried to dodge the question. "Please, just listen to me. You need to let this go, before someone gets hurt."

A frown line appeared between his brows. "You didn't answer me."

"And you're not listening!"

It was rare for me to raise my voice, and Adriano seemed startled. But he regained his composure and said, very calmly, "It was my conflict first. Greco tried to ruin me, and then he came after my family by smashing up Mom's bar. Let's not forget he also kidnapped me, and that Jack got shot in the process." A stray bullet had grazed his arm, but I didn't want to downplay that. He really could have been killed, and we both knew it.

But I had to remind him, "Marcus wasn't even in town when all of that went down." That wasn't new information. My brother had heard it himself from Marcus's crew when they were detaining him. "When I spoke to him on the way to the airport, he said his crew went rogue while he was away, and that he didn't authorize any of that. I believe he was telling the truth."

"Why do you believe that all of a sudden? Did you talk to Greco again, and did he say something to convince you?"

I couldn't admit I'd seen him. I just couldn't. Instead, I said, "I know him, Reno. Anger was clouding my judgement at first, but I can see things clearly now. Yes, he was holding back some crucial information, but that doesn't change the fact that I know the type of man he is. He's just not the monster you're making him out to be."

"You knew him for *a week*."

I shook my head. "Don't dismiss it like it was nothing. How fast did you fall in love with Jack?"

"That's not the same thing."

"No, but my point is, it's possible to care deeply about someone in a short period of time. And it's not like we were casually dating during that week. I had plenty of time to get to know him, because we were together twenty-four/seven and—"

"Don't fucking remind me!" Reno got up and pushed his dark hair out of his eyes. "I know all that, and I'm sure it was intense, and that it felt like you were falling for each other. But he manipulated you, Romy, because that's what sociopaths do! They twist the truth, and they can come across as charming if they choose to, but it's all an act. I'm not blaming you for falling for it. You didn't know better, and—"

Now it was my turn to cut him off. "Please don't make me sound like a naïve little kid. For once, maybe try to see me as an adult and trust my judgement."

His expression softened, and he said, "I do trust your judgement, Romy. But you were fooled by this man—not because you're naïve, but because he's obviously a skilled manipulator. And I'm going to keep looking for him, because that's the only way to be sure he'll never harm any of us again."

A feeling of defeat settled heavily on me. My brother was never going to budge. He just wasn't. As far as he was concerned, he was completely justified in what he was doing, and I was just some pathetic little thing who'd let himself get strung along like a puppet.

I picked up the coffee pot and returned it to the machine as I muttered, "I need to get going. I don't want to be late for that class I told you about."

"Please don't be upset with me," he said. When I turned back to him, there was nothing but sympathy in his eyes. "I love you, Romy, and all I want is to keep you safe. You know that, right?"

I nodded and told him, "I love you, too." I couldn't be mad at him. He was trying so hard to do what he believed was the right thing—protecting me from everyone, even from myself.

I was moody and distracted as I arrived at the dance studio. I kept replaying the conversation with my brother and second-guessing myself—if only I'd said this, or brought up that. Deep down though, I knew it wouldn't have made a difference. Adriano wasn't going to trust my judgement, because when he looked at me, he saw a kid, not a man.

The whole situation felt so hopeless. Would it come down to a choice between my family or Marcus? I didn't want to sacrifice either one—and really, I shouldn't have to. But if Adriano didn't back down, it seemed inevitable.

Instead of sliding deeper into a funk, I tried to shake it off and focus on my surroundings. I was here for some much-needed distraction, after all, so I took a deep breath and tried to focus on the present.

The studio was huge and impressive with polished wood floors, a wall of mirrors, and at least two dozen metal poles mounted floor-to-ceiling. Timothy had been right when he said this place attracted people from all walks of life. A group of three guys in their early twenties were chatting and drinking iced coffee at the far end of the studio. Over by the mirrors, a pair of middle-aged women were putting their hair up, while a mom and her two school-age kids did some stretches. I hadn't realized the class was all-ages. How embarrassing would it be if an eight-year-old could do this but I couldn't?

Pretty soon, I was greeted by a tall, handsome brunet dressed in black workout clothes. He had the body of a professional athlete and moved with so much confidence that I knew right away he had to be the person in charge.

"Come on in," he said, since I was lingering just inside the doorway. "I'm Dare. Welcome to my studio."

"I'm Romy. My friend Timothy is in your ten o'clock class. I told him I'd come and check it out."

Dare nodded. "He called and reserved a spot for you. He also mentioned you were a little nervous, but just remember, everyone is at first. Just go at your own pace, and have fun with it."

He gave me a quick tour of the studio and showed me where to put my things. As I stuck my jacket in a cubby, I tried to make conversation by saying, "Timothy told me you're the founding member of a really successful dance troupe. After working with professionals, what made you want to teach…well, people like me?"

"I get a lot of joy out of showing people what they're capable of."

"Honestly? I don't know if I'm capable of doing this at all."

His green eyes crinkled at the corners when he smiled at me. "Well, then I hope you surprise yourself today."

A moment later, Timothy flung the door open and announced, "I'm here, queens! Let's do this thing!" That was met with enthusiastic greetings from everyone in the studio.

He was dressed all in red, from his cropped T-shirt and leggings with shorts over them to his sneakers and oversized cardigan. When he spotted me, he rushed over and grabbed me in a hug, like we'd known each other for years. "I'm so happy you made it, Romy," he blurted. "I'm not gonna lie, I thought the odds were fifty-fifty that you'd end up blowing it off. But here you are!"

After we did the rounds and he introduced me to everyone, he put his sweater with my jacket and we found a spot to stretch. "How cool is Glynnis? She homeschools her kids, and they do the most amazing activities every week," Timothy said, as he indicated the family of three. "Can you even imagine spending your days learning art, music, and dance when you were their age? I would've been in heaven."

A few more people filtered in while we warmed up, and I was shocked when someone called, "Romy? Is that you?"

I turned toward the voice and spotted a group of five little old ladies in neon-colored leotards, leg warmers, and headbands, as if they'd just escaped from a 1980s Jazzercise video. The one leading the charge toward us was Nana Dombruso, Adriano's grandmother on his dad's side.

She grabbed me in a hug when she reached me and exclaimed, "What a nice surprise! Is your brother taking the class, too?"

The mental image of Adriano trying to pole dance made me grin, and I said, "No, ma'am. I'm here with my new friend Timothy."

"Oh, I know Timmy! In fact, I'm the one who told him about this class." Timothy kissed her cheek, and I was introduced to the rest of Nana's girl gang before she announced, "We're late, so we'd better get ready! Hey, since we have a new student this week, I bet we can talk Dare into performing for us. I just love it when he works that pole!" I had to fight back a laugh.

Once the ladies rushed off to put their coats and handbags away, I said, "I can't believe I just ran into someone I know. How's that even possible, in a city this big?"

"It might be a big city, but within that there's the LGBTQ community, and Nana is our grand dame. She's basically a mega-ally, and a grandma to us all. I met her through my housemates at the pink Victorian, and Nana and Dare go way back, too." Timothy bent at the waist and touched his palms to the floor as he added, "By the way, she's the only person who's allowed to call me Timmy. After I corrected her like, ten times, I finally gave up."

Right before class, Nana succeeded in convincing Dare to do a pole dancing demonstration. I had a feeling she looked for any excuse to get him to do that, and she and her girlfriends were giddy with excitement.

But what followed wasn't strip club-style entertainment. Not by a long shot. Instead, Dare performed like a cross between a ballet dancer and an Olympic gymnast. It was an amazing combination of grace and athleticism, and wow was I intimidated. We obviously weren't supposed to compare ourselves to the expert, but I knew I'd never be that good, not even if I practiced every day for the rest of my life.

Then the class got underway. Dare was joined by two assistants, and we were broken into three sections. Timothy and I were at one end with the beginners, and surprisingly, Nana and her friends were down at the other end with the more experienced students.

The next hour could best be described as humbling. This was only Timothy's second class, but he picked up everything right away. Meanwhile, I flailed, perspired, fell on my ass a few times, and generally made a mess of the whole thing.

To make matters worse, when the class ended, I heard applause from the back of the room. I looked around and sighed when I spotted Adriano and Jack standing with Adriano's half-brother, Dante Dombruso. "I'm thrilled I had an audience for that," I muttered, as I wiped my forehead with the back of my hand.

As I made my way across the studio, I couldn't help but notice the similarities between my brother and Dante. While Adriano and I looked nothing alike, those two were unmistakably brothers. They were both huge guys with dark hair, slightly prominent noses, and strong jawlines, and they were currently sporting matching short beards and very similar black suits.

Adriano had only met Dante and the rest of his dad's family three months ago, but they'd grown close in that short time. I was still processing the fact that he had a bunch of new family members in his life, including four half-brothers. Even though I wasn't related to them at all, the Dombrusos had been trying their best to make me feel included. Meanwhile, I was trying my best not to be completely intimidated by them, especially Dante.

When I reached them, I asked, "What're you doing here?"

"Nana texted us." Adriano pulled his phone from his pocket and held it up so he could read the screen. "And I quote, 'Get your asses down to my dance class pronto! Your cute brother is here, and we all need to go out to lunch after this because I'm ducking hungry.' That text was followed by four more. The first three said 'ducking,' and the last one said 'what the duck!' Autocorrect is clearly winning."

That was hilarious, but I had to remind myself to smile. Since I was supposed to meet Marcus, I tried to think of a good excuse to get out of lunch. The best I could do was, "I'm sweaty and gross, and I'm dressed in ratty workout clothes. I can't go out to eat like this."

Nana joined us just then and exclaimed, "You shouldn't care what people think! If somebody says they don't like the way you're dressed, tell them to kiss your ass! But if you're worried about it, we'll go have lunch at my house instead. I'll call and order up a nice deli platter, and I'll send one of my boys to go get it for us." She pulled a phone out of her bra and started stabbing it with a fingertip and squinting at it, until Jack offered to send the text for her.

There was no graceful way to bow out of this, so I agreed to go before telling them I needed five minutes to clean up a bit. I grabbed my things, and as soon as I was alone in the men's room, I sent a text to Marcus. It said: *I'm so sorry, but I have to cancel seeing you today. I've gotten roped into a family thing and can't get out of it. Can we please try again tomorrow, same place and time?* His reply was sweet and understanding, but I knew he had to be disappointed, just like I was.

Timothy burst into the restroom just then, and I jumped and dropped my phone. Fortunately, it didn't break when it hit the floor. As I picked it up and shoved it in my pocket, he grinned and said, "You're up to something."

"No, I'm not." The fact that my cheeks were burning and probably bright red told a different story.

"You are. Who were you messaging, your ex-boyfriend? I heard a little more of the story last night after you left. Jack didn't go into detail, but I could tell your family really hates this guy."

"Um…"

117

"That's a yes. So, is he even an ex, or have you secretly been seeing him this whole time behind their backs?"

"It's complicated. Please don't tell anyone, okay?"

"I won't say a word, I promise."

"Thanks."

He beamed at me and exclaimed, "This is so romantic! Your true love, spurned by your family, forcing you to carry on in secret— it's like Romeo and Juliet!"

"I don't know why everyone thinks that's romantic," I muttered. "They both die at the end."

∼

Our visit to Nana's house turned into an all-day affair. Several more of her family members came over, and lunch was followed by cocktails and eventually dinner.

It was almost ten p.m. when we finally got back to the townhouse. I said goodnight to Jack and my brother, then went straight to my room to take a shower and put on a clean T-shirt and sweats.

I'd been in bed reading one of Jack's paperbacks for about an hour when my phone vibrated on the night stand. The message from Marcus said: *How was your class this morning?*

I replied: *It was hard and exhausting, and I was even more uncoordinated than I thought I'd be. I'm not sure if I've ever been quite that bad at anything.*

He wrote: *Well, it was worth a try.*

My next message said: *I'm not giving up. I signed up for a month's worth of classes. The next one is on Thursday.*

Marcus responded: *That's great! It didn't sound like you enjoyed it.*

I thought about that before telling him: *I like the challenge. Just because something's hard doesn't mean it's not worth doing.*

His wrote: *Very true.* That was followed by a text that said: *I have a favor to ask. Could I please see you, just for two minutes?*

I replied: *It's a little late for the park.*

His next text almost made me drop my phone: *I know. That's why I'm outside.* Another text popped up a second later: *I just read that and it sounds super creepy. Sorry.*

My heart started racing as I tossed the phone onto the mattress, leapt out of bed, and opened my door. What was he thinking, coming here when my brother was right upstairs?

I paused and listened for a few seconds, hoping to god Jack and Reno were asleep. Since the townhouse was perfectly still, I rushed to the door and opened it as quietly as I could.

Marcus was standing on the porch with a sheepish expression, and I grabbed his wrist and dragged him inside. Then I locked up behind him and speed-walked him to my room.

Once my door was closed and locked behind us, I whispered, "Do you have a death wish?"

"No. I just missed you. I get that this is weird, by the way, and I apologize."

He looked so lost. I didn't know why it hadn't occurred to me sooner, but it finally dawned on me that he had no one in all the world—no one but me. No wonder he'd wanted to see me.

I hugged him, and he sank into it. "Totally worth the risk," he whispered. After a minute, he let go of me and said, "I'll go now, and—"

"No, stay. We'll sneak you out in the morning, before anyone wakes up."

"Are you sure?" When I nodded, he took off his jacket and loafers and slipped into bed with me, still dressed in his T-shirt and jeans.

After I set an alarm on my phone, I turned off the light and drew him into my arms. He fell asleep soon after with his head on my chest, and I held him securely.

When the alarm went off the next morning at six a.m., I fumbled with my phone to shut it off. Then I sat up and looked around. Marcus was long gone, but there was a slip of paper on the nightstand. He'd drawn a picture of two giraffes leaning into each other, along with two words: *thank you.*

17

Romy

For the rest of February, I felt like a double agent. I kept living under my brother's roof, because I thought it was important to stay in the loop about his efforts to find Marcus. I also made several more attempts at talking him out of the manhunt and got nowhere.

At the same time, I kept sneaking off to see Marcus whenever I could. I'd decided to leave sex out of it while we rebuilt our relationship, so we continued to meet at our spot in the park for long walks around the island, picnics, and endless conversations. Some of my favorite afternoons were spent on a blanket at the top of that little island, holding hands and watching the clouds roll by while we talked about anything that came to mind.

Not that everything was perfect during all of this. There was still the constant threat of getting found out, and the thought of how angry and disappointed my brother would be if this came to light wore at me.

Plus, the situation with Art's former associates was still hanging over Marcus. Even though he tried not to let it show, I knew he was worried. Those men were ruthless, and they wouldn't stop until they got what they wanted. It was probably just a matter of time before they made the San Francisco connection and closed in, and then we'd be forced to make some decisions.

Going on the run together was starting to seem like the only option. If my brother wouldn't budge, and if Art's associates tracked Marcus here, San Francisco would become too dangerous for him. As much as I hated running the risk of alienating my family, I cared about Marcus way too much to let him face all of this alone.

It wasn't all sneaking around and stress, though. I also managed to do some perfectly normal things that month, like continuing my pole dancing classes, exploring San Francisco, and spending time with my new friend Timothy.

He was the only person I'd been able to confide in about my secret relationship, and I was grateful to have him to talk to about it. Everyone else I knew, including my friend Pete, was close with my family and would have felt bad keeping secrets from them. But Timothy was on my side, one hundred percent.

On the last Thursday in February, we went out for iced coffee after class. As we took a seat in the crowded coffee house, he asked, "So, have you and your man re-christened your relationship yet?"

"Are you asking if we've had sex since we've been back together?"

"Of course I am! You know I've been waiting on the juicy details."

"No, we haven't. Not yet."

He shot me a look as he took a long drink from his straw. Then he said, "Explain this whole born again virgin thing to me. I mean, you already slept together, and then you decided to rescind the invitation to your ass after you found out he was a lying liar who lied. I guess that makes sense. But it's been *weeks*, and I know you're all team Marcus again. So, what're you waiting for?"

"When we spent that week alone in San Diego, the sex was just really intense."

Timothy raised a brow and dead-panned, "That sounds terrible. I could see why you'd want to avoid that."

"I just want to keep a clear head this time around, instead of letting sex cloud my judgement."

Timothy still looked skeptical. "You know what clouds my judgement? A raging case of blue balls. But you do you, boo."

I grinned and asked, "You get what I'm saying though, don't you?"

"In theory. But I'm still struggling with the notion that you have hot dick on tap and are choosing not to indulge. Aren't you really just punishing yourself?"

"Actually, I've been ready to sleep with him for a while now," I admitted, "but we haven't really had the chance. Whenever I see him, it's just for a couple of hours. That way, I don't have huge blocks of time to account for with my brother."

"Okay, I get it. You don't want a quickie."

"No. I want it to be special." I tried to find a way to explain it and ended up with, "The first time, we fell into bed right away, with the thought that maybe it was just going to be a casual fling. Now that we're a couple, it's going to mean a lot more."

"It'll be like wedding night sex—finally consummating your relationship."

"In a way, yeah." I took a drink of iced coffee before saying, "You know, we talk about my love life a lot, but you never want to talk about yours. Why is that?"

"There's nothing to talk about."

"Really?"

"Oh, believe me," he said, "if there was something happening you'd be getting an earful. But my sex life is just…complicated."

"In what way?"

"Let's say I spot a sexy silver fox at the supermarket. He thinks I'm cute because he's not a dumb-ass, and I'm quite taken by his big zucchini—because we met in the produce section, obviously." He grinned at me and continued, "That mutual attraction isn't enough. Not by a long shot."

"Why not?"

"Because I'm not vanilla. I've tried to make conventional sex— and relationships for that matter—work in the past, but no. I need someone whose kinks align with mine, and the chances of finding that in some random guy on aisle four are pretty freaking slim."

"Okay, I get it. So, where would you normally go to meet someone, a BDSM club?"

"No, although I actually gave the whole BDSM thing a whirl for a while. It wasn't the right fit, either."

"What are you looking for?"

He thought about it before saying, "I want an older guy who's in charge, but I don't want a Dom or a daddy. It's hard to describe exactly what I need from him, but I'll know it when I see it."

"Well, I hope you find what you're looking for."

He raised his drink in a toast and said, "You and me both, my friend."

I had plans to meet Marcus at our usual spot that afternoon, so after my coffee break with Timothy, I took a cab to Golden Gate Park. I'd gotten in the habit of getting dropped off on the main road, then taking a nice stroll past the boathouse to the Chinese pavilion, where he'd be waiting for me.

I was deep in thought as I took that stroll. My conversation with Timothy had gotten me thinking about how many things had to align for Marcus and me to meet. But I was pulled back to the present when a deep voice said, "Hi, Romy."

When I looked up, I had to stop myself from audibly gasping. Dante Dombruso was directly ahead of me, and so totally out of his element that I almost couldn't process seeing him here. He was the type of man who wore expensive suits for just about any occasion, but now he was dressed in jeans and a black polo shirt, and it just seemed wrong.

Since he'd been working closely with Adriano to find Marcus, my heart leapt and my gaze immediately shot past him to the lake. Had we been discovered, or was this just some sort of weird coincidence?

As panic welled up in me, I blurted, "What are you doing here?"

"My husband and I are babysitting our grandson today, so we decided to bring him to the park. We were going to rent a paddle boat, but they're closed." He studied me curiously and asked, "Is everything alright?"

I tried my best to maintain a poker face as I said, "Yeah, fine. You just startled me."

Meanwhile, my mind was racing. What if Marcus hadn't arrived yet? I was a little early, so he could come walking up at any moment. If he spotted him, Dante would go straight to Adriano, and everything would fall apart.

There were all sorts of ramifications to Adriano finding out about us, of course. But what really struck me in that moment was the very real possibility of ruining my relationship with my brother. The thought made me nauseous.

Yes, I'd made the choice to lie, and to sneak around behind his back. It had almost felt like a game, but this was a huge wakeup call. Would Adriano ever forgive me, if and when the truth came out? Did I even deserve his forgiveness?

I needed to fix this—all of this—before it was too late. But how?

Just then, Dante's grandson ran up and tugged on his sleeve. I was incredibly grateful for the distraction. When I said, "Hi there, Malik," the little boy grew shy and hid behind Dante's leg. We'd met at a family function, but he didn't seem to remember me.

A moment later, Dante's husband Charlie joined him, gesturing at Malik as he announced, "The potty break was a success." Then he spotted me rooted in place a few feet away and flashed me a smile. "Hey there, Romy. What're you doing here?"

Even though my heartbeat was drumming in my ears, I tried to sound casual when I said, "I've been coming to the park to walk for a few weeks now. I don't belong to a gym here in San Francisco, so it's a good way to get some exercise." One of the first things I'd had to learn as an EMT was how to seem calm and collected, even when everything was falling apart around me. Right then, I was very grateful for that skill.

Dante was shrewd and observant though, and I could tell he wasn't totally buying it. "Isn't this pretty far out of your way?"

"Sure, but it's gorgeous here. We don't have anything like this in Vegas." All true.

The little boy decided he'd had enough of not being the center of attention at that point and exclaimed, "You said we could see buff-lows!" It seemed like he was on the verge of pitching a huge fit.

"We're on our way," Charlie promised, as he scooped up the child. "Good to see you, Romy."

He hurried toward the parking lot, but Dante stayed where he was and said, "Dealing with a five-year-old is like trying to negotiate a peace treaty with a warlord. We almost had a major meltdown after we promised paddleboats and couldn't deliver. All I could think of to distract him was offering to go see the buffaloes, because I remembered there were some in the park. They damn well better still be there, or else we're screwed."

It really felt like he was making an excuse to keep the conversation going. Maybe he was waiting for me to slip up, because he could tell I was hiding something. Or maybe that was just my guilty conscience talking.

I stuck a smile on my face and said, "I'm pretty sure the buffaloes are right where they've always been. Good luck, though."

Dante murmured, "Thanks." He still seemed suspicious, and he paused for a moment before saying, "See you, Romy." Finally, he headed toward the parking lot.

I started walking in the opposite direction, but as soon as he was out of sight, I broke into a run. Once I'd ducked around the corner of the boat house, I pulled my phone from my pocket. My hands were shaking, so it was all I could do to fire off a quick text to Marcus, warning him about Dante. Then I started pacing, as worry twisted my gut.

He called me two or three minutes later and said, "Thanks for the warning. I'd been just about to pull into the parking lot when I got your text."

"Where are you now?"

"I thought it was best to leave the park, so I'm on Fulton Street, at Eighteenth."

"Stay there. I'll come to you."

After we disconnected the call, I took off running. It seemed to take forever to cut across the park, but in reality it was just a few minutes until I emerged onto the street.

The rented black sports car was right where he said it'd be. I climbed into the passenger seat, and when I grabbed Marcus in a hug, he murmured, "Baby, you're shaking."

"That was such a close call. I really thought we'd be okay there, because no one I knew would come to the lake. But I was totally wrong."

"It's alright now," he said, as he rubbed my back.

"But we can't come back here. It doesn't feel safe anymore."

"Then we'll figure something else out. For right now though, where can I take you?"

"Your hotel. Maybe I'm getting paranoid, but I feel exposed sitting out here like this." He nodded before starting the engine.

$\sim$

Marcus was staying in a contemporary high rise hotel near the financial district. Since I was already rattled, the fact that it was crowded and hectic set my nerves on edge. "It's not usually like this," he told me, as he put a protective arm around my shoulders and guided me through the bustling lobby. There was a sign near the elevators welcoming some sort of convention, which probably explained the chaos.

It was a relief when we reached his suite. As soon as the door shut behind us, I buried my face in his chest, and he put his arms around me and asked, "What do you need, Romy?"

"First, I'd like to get cleaned up." The sweat had cooled on my skin, making me shiver. "But we have to make a plan, Marcus. We can't—"

"One thing at a time. Go take a nice, long shower, and I'll meet you on the couch when you're done."

I made my way to the bathroom and stripped down quickly before stepping under a stream of very hot water. As it ran over my back and shoulders, I braced my hands against the white tile wall and worked on letting myself relax.

Afterwards, I dried off and put on the fluffy white bathrobe that was hanging on the back of the door. The feeling of the soft terrycloth against my skin caused a déjà vu sensation, momentarily transporting me back to the week we'd spent together in San Diego.

But so much had changed since then. Over the past month, we'd built trust and really gotten to know each other. A solid relationship had developed.

And along the way, I'd fallen deeply in love with Marcus.

Not that I'd said those words to him—not yet, anyway. I told myself it was a timing thing, that I was worried he'd think it was too soon. Things were going so well, and I didn't want to mess it up. But really, my fear was that he wasn't there yet. What if I told him I loved him and just got a thank you in return? It was scary to put myself out there, so I'd been holding back.

I sighed at my reflection in the mirror above the sink. Even though I'd been working on building my confidence, I clearly still had a way to go.

After quickly finger-combing my hair, I left the bathroom and went to find Marcus. He was right where he said he'd be—waiting for me on the couch in the sleek black and tan living room. I climbed onto his lap as he said, "If you want anything, I could order room service. Would you like some tea? Or…soup? I don't know what would make you feel better."

"I'm okay, but thank you for wanting to take care of me."

"I don't really know what I'm doing," he admitted. "It's not like I have a lot of experience with this kind of thing."

When I told him, "You're doing great," that definitely made him happy. "What about you, Marcus? Do you need anything?"

"Just you."

"You've already got me."

A smile spread across his handsome face. "Yeah?"

I grinned and nodded. "So, what are you going to do with me?"

"If it was up to me, I'd take you to bed and make love to you for hours. But like you said, we need to make some plans, and—"

I cut him off with a deep kiss before saying, "The plans can wait." Just in case that was too subtle, I untied the sash and let the robe slip off my shoulders. That caused a sigh of pleasure, and he slid his hands up my back as he kissed my neck.

Everything happened very quickly after that. He carried me to the bedroom, and as soon as we were both naked he began to feast on me. There was no other way to describe it. He worked me into a frenzy with his mouth and tongue and fingers, until I was writhing on the mattress and begging him to fuck me.

When he replaced the three fingers in my ass with his cock, I muttered, "Fuck yes."

Somehow, I managed to keep him in me as I rolled us over. Then I began riding him hard, slamming my ass onto his cock as I braced my hands on his shoulders. I knew I'd be sore later, but I welcomed it—I wanted the ache to remind me of this hours from now, when I was alone in bed and missing the feeling of him deep inside me.

"You're so beautiful, Romy," he told me, in a voice as rough as gravel. I looked into his eyes and saw wonder there, and bliss. And there was that electric connection, burning brighter than ever and making me feel like he was a part of me.

He grinned and flipped me onto my back. As he held my legs up and slid his cock into me, I teased, "Oh, of course. You just had to be in charge."

He chuckled at that. "You and I both know you're the one in charge. I just needed to switch positions, so I could do this." He shifted a bit and started nailing my prostate with each thrust, and my laugh morphed into a yell of intense pleasure.

Neither of us lasted very long after that. I came first, and maybe thirty seconds later he growled as he pumped his load into my ass. Afterwards, we were both gasping for air as he slid out of me and dropped onto the mattress.

As if on cue, we rolled over to face each other, and he took my hand. For a minute or two, all either of us could do was catch our breath. Finally, he murmured, "I missed that."

"Me, too."

"I mean, I'm glad we took things slowly this past month—"

"Same," I said. "But I'm so glad we're back to where we were."

"Actually, we're not. This is something new."

I nodded. "You're right. It's like…"

Marcus finished my sentence for me. "Like there aren't any barriers between us. I think I was holding back before, when I knew I was keeping this huge secret and was so afraid of what the truth would do to us."

"But now, it feels like a new beginning."

He kissed my knuckle, and then he held my hand to his chest and said, "Exactly."

18

Marcus

Our afternoon was perfection. Romy and I ended up making love twice, and in between we cuddled, and talked, and just enjoyed each other's company. He even stayed for dinner before finally glancing at the time. I could tell he felt guilty when he said, "I'm so sorry, but I have to go. My brother's going to wonder what happened to me."

Even though I wanted to beg him to make up literally any excuse and spend the night with me, I tried to play it cool. "I know, baby, and it's fine," I said. "I'll request a ride share for you while you get dressed." He was wearing a white bathrobe, and I loved the way it kept slipping down and revealing his bare shoulder.

All too soon, both of us were fully clothed and stalling for time at the door. "I'll text you tomorrow," he said, as he lightly traced my jaw. "Maybe we should meet here again, since I can't really think of another place with guaranteed privacy."

"Sure. Whatever you want."

"And we'll come up with a plan, someplace we can go where no one knows us and we won't have to sneak around." He searched my eyes as he added, "Somewhere safe. I was thinking Seattle, maybe? Neither of us has any ties to that city, so if we went there we'd be able to disappear…"

He was trying to talk himself into this, but there was a lot to consider. "What about your family, Romy?"

"I'll stay in touch, of course, and I can come back and visit."

"But how do you think that'll go over? Will your brother just welcome you back with open arms if he knows you ran off with me?"

"I...I don't know."

I had no idea how this was ever going to get resolved. As much as I disliked his brother, I understood what he meant to Romy, and I really didn't want to tear them apart. At the same time, I needed Romy like I needed air, so no fucking way was I just going to bow out and make his decision for him.

But something had to give. Not only was sneaking around behind his brother's back a disaster waiting to happen, I really needed to keep moving. I'd been lucky so far, but Art's former friends and associates would figure out I was in San Francisco eventually, just like they'd figured out Vegas. They had plenty of manpower and resources, enough to turn this city upside down and shake it until I fell out.

All I could do for now was gather Romy in an embrace and try to sound confident as I told him, "We'll figure this out tomorrow."

He nodded and tried to sound confident, too. "We will."

"Your Lyft is going to be here any minute. Want me to walk you downstairs?"

"No, thanks. The lobby's probably still crowded, so I'd rather say goodbye here, in private."

As we lingered over a kiss, I memorized him with all my senses. The taste of his mouth. His clean, familiar scent. The softness of his hair beneath my fingertips. That little mewl he made as he deepened the kiss. That way, I could replay this moment once he was gone and I was all alone in this impersonal hotel room.

Eventually, he stepped back and opened the door. There was longing in his eyes. I tried to memorize every last detail of the way he looked. Some sort of goodbye was exchanged, but I barely registered what was said.

And then he was gone, and it felt like all the color had drained from the world.

I went to the bedroom, tangled myself up in the blankets and pillows, and breathed in his scent. But instead of offering me comfort, it just made me miss him even more.

As I stared at the ceiling, I asked myself yet again who I'd been before Romy came into my life. I couldn't even comprehend it now —all those meaningless nights and days, spent in that endless hustle. I'd come to realize it hadn't just been about Art and meeting his expectations. I'd let myself get caught up in the game, and I'd tried to convince myself that it mattered—the money, the power, the trappings of success. I'd allowed that world to become my life, because I didn't have anything else to care about.

It all seemed so empty, so pointless, compared to the way I felt with Romy. He was what I lived for now, and I loved him more than anything in this entire world.

I wanted to tell him that, but I didn't know how. I'd never loved anyone before, and I'd sure as hell never said those words out loud. But it seemed to me that the timing of it was important, and it made sense to let him set the pace. Until then, I'd just have to be patient and try my damnedest not to fuck this up.

Several hours later, I'd forgotten about the book in my hand and was staring at the ceiling again. My heart leapt when my phone buzzed, because I thought Romy might have messaged me. But then I saw it was from an unknown number.

The text turned out to be from one of Art's former friends and associates, an annoying little weasel of a man. I could only assume he'd gotten my number from one of the dirtbags I used to employ in Vegas. It said: *Mario, my boy, it's Norton Gileki. We need to talk. A lot of people are looking for you, and they're pretty pissed off.*

As if I didn't know he was at the top of that list. He'd gone ballistic when he found out Art had left me the majority of his assets. Ever since then, he'd been telling anyone who'd listen that he was owed that money, and that he intended to get his hands on it one way or another.

Another text popped up from the same number: *I can help. Meet me at the R and J Tavern in an hour.*

That was followed by an address. A cold trickle of dread rolled down my spine when I realized it was in San Francisco.

Fucking hell—they'd found me.

I got up and began to pace. What was my next move? Should I run, or stand my ground and confront Gileki?

If I had people to back me up, I'd definitely confront him. No question. But putting a crew together wasn't even an option in San Francisco, because it would immediately alert the Dombruso family to my presence.

So now here I was, on my own and facing a tough decision. Gileki himself wasn't a threat, but he'd obviously bring muscle to the meeting. I wasn't too worried about his bodyguards though, because he'd asked to meet in public. If his plan was to abduct and torture me until I gave up my offshore bank accounts, he really wouldn't pick someplace with witnesses.

And I could see why he'd want to meet. He had a very high opinion of himself and his skills as a negotiator, so he might actually believe he could convince me to give him a cut of the money. Not that Art had left him high and dry. He'd actually made a point of leaving very generous sums to all his friends and associates, including Gileki. But that was the thing about greed—no amount was ever enough.

While I was pacing, another text popped up: *So, you coming or what?*

I replied: *Give me one good reason why I should take this meeting.*

His response said: *Because I hear you could use some friends, kid. The other men looking for you aren't going to be reasonable like me, but I'm willing to make you an offer. Cut me in on what Art left you, and my people become your people.*

That was actually a pretty compelling argument. Gileki ran a huge crew out of New York, and in a lot of ways, teaming up with him made sense. The two other men looking for me, Berger and

Romano, had a certain degree of respect for Gileki. If I got him on my side and got his numbers behind me, they'd back off. I was sure of it.

I sent another message confirming the meeting, and then I tossed my phone onto the bed and exhaled slowly. There was a chance this was a huge mistake, but it felt like a calculated risk. I had a lot to potentially gain from this meeting. Plus, I couldn't keep dodging these men forever. Sooner or later, I'd have to take a stand, show them I wasn't going to be intimidated, and put an end to this game of cat and mouse. Tonight was as good a time as any.

After checking the time, I went and changed into my best suit. Then I opened the bottom drawer of the dresser and found the brown paper bag I'd hidden under some sweats.

Inside it was the Glock I'd purchased the week before.

I checked the handgun's clip to confirm it was loaded. Then I tucked it into the back of my waistband and straightened my posture.

My thoughts went to Romy, and I had to push down all the emotions that suddenly threatened to overwhelm me. I'd walked into countless dangerous situations over the years, and I'd barely given it a second thought. But this felt completely different, because it wasn't just about me anymore. For the first time in my life, I had someone who cared about me, and who'd be devastated if I died tonight.

And for the first time, I had something to live for.

It was so tempting to bail out of this meeting, to go to Romy and beg him to run away with me. We could go anywhere in the world. We could disappear.

But running wasn't the answer. Resolving this once and for all was.

"I'm doing this for us, baby," I whispered.

Then I took a deep breath and pulled up my game face. It was time to step back into Mario Greco's world.

19

Marcus

The bar where I was meeting Gileki didn't look like anything special, just your basic neighborhood tavern. The only window was heavily tinted so I couldn't get a look inside, but the place didn't immediately raise any red flags.

After driving past it in my rental car to check it out, I circled the block and selected a parking space behind the building. San Francisco was continually becoming more upscale and expensive, but gentrification hadn't reached this industrial neighborhood on the outskirts of town. There was litter and graffiti just about everywhere I looked, and the whole place had a sense of neglect.

I was on high alert as I walked around to the front of the tavern, but everything was perfectly still. Once I reached the door, I squared my shoulders and set my expression to one of cold indifference before stepping inside.

The shabby room was one long rectangle, with a bar to my left and a few booths in the back. Except for some music playing in the background, it was oddly quiet.

Maybe half a dozen men were seated at the bar. I strode past it, moving deeper into the building. After a moment, I spotted Gileki seated in a booth in the back corner. He was fidgeting with an empty highball glass, and when we made eye contact, he quickly looked away.

Something was wrong.

My pulse sped up as I stopped in my tracks and looked around. Where was the bartender? And why were all the patrons big, muscular guys?

The man immediately to my left was tense. I could sense it even with his back to me. That was when it finally dawned on me—we weren't meeting in public at all. Gileki had taken over the entire tavern.

It was a trap.

I turned around and was about to bolt for the door when it opened and two older men stepped inside. Romano grinned at me while Berger said, "You've been a real pain in the ass, Mario, making us hunt for you like we got nothing better to do with our time. I'm gonna make sure you pay for that. Not that I can kill you until you fork over Art's money, of course, but I can sure as hell make you wish you were dead."

It felt like time slowed down over the next few seconds. Berger started to reach into his jacket, and I grabbed the big guy next to me by the shoulders and pulled him backwards, so he fell into the aisle and blocked it. Then I sprinted toward the back of the room.

Shots rang out. It felt like my shoulder suddenly caught fire. I staggered a few steps, but I didn't stop. I couldn't. If I stopped, I was dead.

Everything sped up again, and I began acting on pure survival instinct. I grabbed the gun from my waistband and used its hilt to break the nose of a huge guy who'd stepped in front of me. As I dodged around him, someone up ahead shot at me. A searing pain radiated from my left side. I returned fire and was vaguely aware of him falling to the floor, just as another man grabbed my arm. I landed a punch and managed to shake him loose before propelling myself forward.

By some miracle, I managed to reach a door at the very back of the bar, which led to a store room. I slammed it behind me and knocked over a wire rack to slow down my pursuers, then wove through a maze of boxes before launching myself out the rear exit.

Fear and adrenaline spurred me on as I sprinted down a dark alley. The pain in my shoulder and side were worse than anything I'd ever experienced, but I couldn't think about that now. I just needed to keep moving.

Finally, I dove into the rental car and started the engine. Several gunshots rang out behind me as I threw it into gear and slammed on the gas. A bullet shattered my rear window, but I didn't look back.

The tires squealed as I took a series of quick turns. I fully expected to hear sirens at any moment, but even though I knew I wasn't being followed, I couldn't slow down. I might only have a few minutes left before I bled out, and it was vitally important to reach my destination.

I had to get to Romy. I needed to tell him I loved him.

I needed to see him one more time before I died.

Nothing else mattered.

Nothing but him.

20

Romy

When I went to get something to drink in the middle of the night, I was surprised to find Jack sitting at the kitchen table. He looked up from his paperback and asked, "Couldn't sleep either?"

"No. I just have a lot on my mind."

"Anything you want to talk about?" I shook my head, and he gestured toward the stove. "The kettle's still hot. Why don't you make yourself a cup of tea and join me?"

As I took a mug from the cupboard, I asked, "Good book?"

"It's great. I'll lend it to you when I'm done."

We chatted for a few minutes, until a knock at the door interrupted us. He muttered, "Who'd be dropping by this late? It's after midnight."

"I'll go see."

There was nobody on the porch when I glanced through the peep hole, but I opened the door anyway, so I could take a look outside. The first thing I saw was Marcus's rental car. It was at an odd angle and partially up on the sidewalk, and the driver's side door was open.

"Romy."

I stepped outside at the sound of my name, and there he was.

Marcus's complexion was ashen as he leaned against the house to the left of the doorway. He was clutching his side, and his hand was covered in blood.

Fear and panic jolted through me as I blurted, "What happened?"

"I was shot."

He leaned on me heavily as I guided him into the foyer. As soon as we made it over the threshold, he collapsed onto the floor, and I yelled, "Somebody help us!"

I ripped open his shirt, and then I pulled off my T-shirt and pressed it against the wound below his ribcage to slow the bleeding. Meanwhile, Jack raced into the room, and my brother ran downstairs with his phone in his hand and froze on the last step. "Call 911," I yelled. "We need an ambulance!"

Marcus struggled to sit up as he blurted, "No! You can't."

"We have to," I told him, as I discovered a second wound near his collarbone and pressed my palm to it. "You're losing a lot of blood, and we need to get you to a hospital."

"I can't. Please." His voice was growing weaker. "I returned fire. I don't know if I killed someone tonight, and I can't go back to jail. I just can't. If I went to a hospital with a gunshot wound, they'd call the police."

"But you need help, Marcus. You need—"

His breathing was becoming labored, and there was agony in his eyes when his gaze locked with mine. "I just need one thing, baby. I need to tell you I love you. I should have told you sooner. I love you, Romy. God, I love you. You're my whole world, and I'm so fucking sorry for all the mistakes I made."

"I love you too, Marcus, and I have to help you. We need an ambulance."

"Please don't cry, baby." I didn't realize I was until he reached up with a shaky hand and tried to wipe away my tears. "I just needed you to know how I felt before I..."

"You're not going to die! I won't let you." I looked over my shoulder at my brother. He was still on that bottom step, and he was holding his phone to his ear. "Please, Reno," I begged, "help us. I love him so much, and I can't lose him. I just can't!"

Adriano came over to me and crouched down so we were at eye-level. "I am. I just called for help."

"No." Marcus struggled to sit up again. His voice was little more than a whisper. "I can't go back to prison. Please."

"I didn't call 911," Adriano told him. "I called my older brother. Dante's sending a medical team as we speak."

Marcus slumped in relief and whispered, "Thank you."

But I shook my head and insisted, "We have to get him to a hospital."

"In any other circumstances, yes. But he's right," my brother told me. "They'll call the police for a gunshot wound, it's standard procedure. And if he killed whoever he shot at tonight, he'll go to jail for murder."

"I can't," Marcus whispered, as his eyes slid shut. "I can't go back to prison. Please, Romy."

A sob tore from me as his body went limp. I quickly felt for his pulse, and when I found it I whispered, "Thank god."

My mind was racing as I looked around. Even though I was trained for this, it was so hard to think clearly when the man I loved was bleeding out in front of me. Adriano was totally focused though, and he asked, "How can I help?"

Jack raced back into the foyer with an armload of towels and a first aid kit. I hadn't even realized he'd left. I grabbed a towel and pressed it to Marcus's shoulder as I told my brother, "Come around to his right side and apply steady pressure to this spot. He won't make it unless we can stop the bleeding." While Adriano followed my instructions, I asked him, "How far out is whoever Dante's sending?"

"Less than five minutes. Luckily, they live nearby."

"Are they equipped to deal with this type of emergency?"

"This is exactly what they do."

"Who are these people?"

"One's an MD who was also a field medic in Afghanistan.

Dante said he's helped the family on more than one occasion. He's also bringing his husband, who's a nurse."

While we were talking, I replaced the blood-soaked T-shirt with a towel and checked Marcus's pulse again. Then I leaned over to listen to his breathing. That was when I noticed a pool of blood seeping out from beneath his shoulder. "There must be both an entry and exit wound," I said. "Help me raise him up, so I can wedge a towel underneath him."

Just as we finished doing that, a bearded man in his fifties rushed through the open front door carrying a large medical bag. "I'm Doctor Pope. Dante Dombruso sent me," he said, as he dropped to his knees beside Marcus and took off his overcoat. He was wearing pajamas underneath. "What can you tell me about this man's injuries?"

While Adriano and I kept up the pressure on the wounds to try to stop the blood loss, I quickly recited what I knew. As the doctor pulled on a pair of rubber gloves, he glanced at me and asked, "Are you a paramedic?"

"I used to be an EMT."

An Asian man in his thirties came in just then, rolling a large crash cart. He was wearing a trench coat over a pair of dark blue pajamas which matched the doctor's, and he immediately went to work setting up the cart.

As Dr. Pope began checking Marcus's vital signs, he asked me, "Do you know his blood type? With this much blood loss, there's no question we'll need to do a transfusion."

I shook my head, but Adriano said, "I'm a universal donor, so you can use my blood."

That surprised me, and I asked my brother, "Why would you want to help Marcus?"

"Because I love you," he said matter-of-factly, "and you love him."

～

Around dawn, after he'd been moved by stretcher to my room, I stood at Marcus's bedside and held his hand. Sedatives and antibiotics dripped steadily from an IV, while a portable monitor displayed his vital signs. He was pale and had been through hell, but he was alive. It felt like an absolute miracle.

After a while, Dante came into the room carrying a chair. He and his husband had arrived shortly after the doctor, but I'd been so focused on what was happening with Marcus that we'd barely said two words to each other.

I thanked him and took a seat when he placed the chair beside me, and then I asked, "Where's my brother?"

"He and Jack are cleaning up the foyer. It looks like a murder scene."

I'd barely noticed. After a moment, I said, "Thanks for sending that doctor to us. He was really something."

"Yeah, he's a rock star."

"I'm just curious why you'd help Marcus, after spending the last month or so trying to find him and kill him."

"I was helping *you*, because Adriano asked me to. And we weren't going to kill him," Dante said. "We just wanted to talk to him and make it clear that he was done messing with our family." I shot him an incredulous look, and he admitted, "Okay, so maybe we were going to smack him around a bit, to get our point across. But that's it."

"But that's over now, right?"

He nodded. Then he pulled a gun from the back of his waistband and removed the clip before checking the chamber. "A couple things before I take off. This was in your boyfriend's rental car, which is now with a mechanic friend of mine. He's going to fix the busted back window and the bullet holes, because it looked like a felony on wheels."

He placed the emptied gun on the dresser and pulled Marcus's phone from his pocket. As he put it next to the gun, he said, "I also had someone hack into your boyfriend's phone to check his messages. That's how we figured out where he went last night. I sent my brother Vincent to clean up the crime scene, so there's no evidence of what went down there. He also did some digging, and it turns out the guy Marcus shot is alive. He had the sense not to go to a hospital, and the doc-for-hire that patched him up expects him to make a full recovery."

"How'd you find that out?"

"We have a lot of connections in this town," Dante said. "Ask the right people, and you can get just about any answer you need."

"I'm surprised you did all that."

"Adriano asked me to help you, so that's what I did. What good would it do to patch up your boyfriend, only for him to get thrown in jail?"

It was both amazing and slightly alarming to realize just how easily Dante could make a crime disappear if he wanted to. "Thank you again. I can't even tell you how much I appreciate all your help."

He shrugged, as if he hadn't just worked a series of miracles. "That's what this family does, we look after our own." I didn't bother reminding him I wasn't actually a Dombruso, because that detail didn't seem to matter to him. Then he said, "Alright, I'm out of here. Charlie's about to fall asleep, so I need to get him to bed."

After he left, I moved my chair closer to Marcus's bedside and checked his pulse, even though it was already displayed on the monitor. Then I began stroking his hair as I said softly, "I love you so much, and I was terrified, Marcus. My god, what if I'd lost you?"

"Why didn't you tell me how you felt about him?"

The voice from the doorway startled me. I glanced at Adriano, who was leaning against the doorframe. He looked exhausted, and there was a gauze bandage around his arm, from the blood donation that had saved my boyfriend's life. "You'd already made up your mind about him, so I didn't think it would make a difference."

"It does. But shit, Romy, this is really tough for me. Even knowing what he means to you, I just don't think I can trust him."

"Then trust me instead. I love you, Reno, and I'm so grateful for the way you've always had my back. But I really wish you'd try to see me for who I am, instead of who I was. I'm not a naïve little kid anymore. I'm a full-grown adult, and you can trust my judgement."

"I know that. But what if he hurts you?"

"He won't." My brother looked skeptical, so I said, "Instead of taking my word for who he is, please just talk to him when he's well enough. Get to know him. Also, find out why he started that feud with you in the first place. Here's a hint—it goes back about five and a half years."

"But I only met him for the first time a year ago."

"No, you didn't. Let him tell you the story, and put yourself in his shoes. Try to factor in where he was coming from, too. He got locked up at nineteen and spent nearly ten years in federal prison for a crime he didn't commit. He'd only been out about six months when you two first met. All he knew how to do was act tough, because that was how he learned to survive."

"I promise I'll listen to what he has to say."

I got up and crossed the room to him, and as I gave my brother a hug I said, "Thank you for that, and for everything you did tonight. I'm so grateful."

"You're welcome. I love you, kid."

"I love you, too." I stepped back and grinned. "Maybe it's time to stop calling me 'kid' though."

"Yeah, maybe. I really need to get some sleep now, and so do you. I'll see you in a few hours."

After he left, I returned to Marcus and kissed his forehead. "I think my brother's coming around," I whispered. "In fact, I wouldn't be surprised if you and he ended up being friends one day." Then I settled in at his bedside, so I could look after him while he slept.

21

Marcus

I awoke gradually, swimming up through a haze of painkillers and sedatives. That was my guess anyway, but it was probably a good one. I remembered the agony I'd been in after I was shot, and since I wasn't hurting anymore, I could only assume a lot of pharmaceuticals were involved.

It took a while to open my eyes, and even more time to focus on the light fixture in the center of the ceiling. Then I shut them again and waited for the brain fog to clear.

Where was I? This place didn't feel or smell like a hospital. I tried opening my eyes again and turned my head. What I saw filled me with joy.

Romy was curled up in a chair right beside the bed, sound asleep and tucked under a fuzzy blanket. He was achingly beautiful. More than that—he was ethereal. I remembered thinking that the first time I saw him, and I'd been right.

I tried to say his name, but my mouth and throat were so dry that I could barely make a sound. Instead, I watched him sleep and was reminded of the very first night we'd spent together. At that point, I'd been the one keeping a vigil at his bedside before finally nodding off in the early morning hours.

It was astonishing to think about how far we'd come as a couple since then, and how much I'd changed. In a lot of ways, it felt like I'd finally started living the day I met Romy.

His eyelids fluttered. Then he raised them halfway. As soon as his gaze focused on me, he became fully awake and hurled himself out of the chair as he shouted my name.

While he gingerly went in for a hug, I managed to rasp, "Hi, baby."

"How do you feel?"

"Drugged."

He nodded. "The doctor gave you a sedative. It's probably still working its way out of your system."

A moment later, a deep voice asked, "Is everything alright?" Fear trickled down my spine when I raised my head and saw Adriano Dombruso standing in the doorway.

While I tried to decide if I was capable of sitting up, let alone defending myself, Romy turned to him and said, "Everything's great. Could you please do me a favor and bring him a glass of water?"

From my perspective, that felt exactly like a fluffy kitten asking a bristling hell hound to go and run an errand for him. The hell hound nodded and shot me a look before turning and walking away.

As soon as he was gone, I tried to sit up, which sent a sharp jolt of pain through me. "You need to stay still," Romy said, as he brushed my hair off my forehead. "You were shot twice and stitched back up by a mob doctor. The good news is, the bullets missed your internal organs, but your body needs time to heal, sweetheart."

My voice sounded like gravel when I whispered, "I like it when you call me that." That earned me the sweetest smile.

When his brother returned, I tensed up again. He and I maintained eye contact as he went around to Romy's side of the bed and handed him a glass with a straw in it. After he left again, Romy helped me swallow a couple of pain pills, and then he told me, "You're safe here, Marcus, and everything's going to be okay."

"But I shot someone." A lot of the night before was a blur, but parts of it were starting to come back into focus.

"He survived, and the police aren't looking for you."

I muttered, "Thank god." A minute or two later, I let the need to sleep overtake me.

22

Marcus

For the next few days, just about all I did was sleep. Romy stayed with me around the clock, and the doctor came by and checked on me twice a day, but everyone else left us alone. I suspected the last part was because Romy had asked his family to give me some time.

Finally, when I was a bit stronger, he said, "My brother's been wanting to talk to you."

"Yeah, I figured. I've been dreading it."

"It's going to be okay, because Adriano understands what we mean to each other. He saw it first-hand when you showed up here to tell me you loved me, with what you thought was your dying breath." He sighed and added, "I still can't believe you came here, instead of driving yourself to a hospital. You should have prioritized saving your life over everything else."

"I'll always come to you, Romy," I said softly, "*always*, especially if I'm hurt or scared. I'll run to you because you're home to me, and the only person in this world who makes me feel safe."

He grasped my face between his palms and kissed me before whispering, "I love you so much."

Every time he said those words, it felt like the best gift I'd ever received. I reached up and touched his cheek as I told him, "I love you, too. More than anything."

A little while later, his brother appeared in the open doorway. Romy told me, "I'm going to give you two some privacy." When I nodded, he kissed my cheek and whispered, "It's going to be fine. You'll see."

Adriano only took a couple of steps into the room before pausing and crossing his arms over his chest. Then he started to say something, but I blurted, "I'm so fucking sorry. I know those words don't change anything, but I really am, and I wish none of it had happened—your fiancé getting shot, you getting abducted, your mom's bar getting wrecked. I lost control of my men, and it's totally my fault. If I'd gotten them to respect me the way I should have, they never would have acted without my permission. Everything they did is all on me, and if you want to take me outside and beat the living shit out of me, I won't fight back."

A frown creased his brow. "I'm not going to do that, Marcus. Never mind that you're recovering from a serious injury. Romy would never forgive me." A few moments ticked by. Finally, he told me, "Romy says we met about five years ago. I don't remember it."

"Long story short, I was brought to your club by some thug I was trying to impress, and you had your men throw me out because I looked exactly like what I was—an angry, classless little punk. I was humiliated and really fucking pissed off, and I carried that grudge for years. So, when I saw the opportunity to lash out at you by trying to take over your illegal gambling operation, I jumped at it. But I don't blame you for keeping me out of your club. Not anymore. If I'd been in your position, I probably would have done the same thing."

His frown deepened. "Am I really supposed to believe all this? You're sorry, you've changed, you understand my perspective all of a sudden?"

"No. I figure you'll always think I'm full of shit, just like you'll always believe I'm not good enough for Romy. You're totally right about that second thing, by the way. I'm *not* good enough for him, not by a long shot. He's an absolute angel, and the best person I've ever known. But I love him, and all I can do is learn, and grow, and try my damnedest to become even a fraction of the man he deserves."

Now Adriano looked frustrated. "I really wanted to yell and cuss you out, but you're making that tough by being so fucking contrite."

"Sorry. I'll shut up now. Go ahead and cuss me out."

He didn't know what to say to that, so after a few moments, he went a different route. "I don't trust you. I doubt I ever will. But Romy does. He loves you and wants to be with you, which means you're a part of this family now. To be clear though, I've got my eye on you. If you ever hurt him or any other member of my family, I'll fucking tear you apart with my bare hands."

"That's fair."

He sighed, and his posture relaxed, just a little. "You've taken all the fun out of this. I thought it'd be so satisfying to finally tell you off." I started to say something, but he cut me off with a sharp glare. "Don't fucking apologize again. I'm going to go get Romy and let him know we're done, for now."

Adriano started to leave, but then he turned back and said, "I almost forgot. I need you to make a list of all the people who've been coming after you, not just the ones who ambushed you the night you got shot."

"No problem, but can I ask why?"

"Since you're a part of this family now, you're under our protection. We Dombrusos look out for our own. My brother Dante and his associates are going to make sure your enemies understand this and leave you alone."

The sense of relief was overwhelming. That ongoing problem with Art's associates had been hanging over me for such a long time, with no solution in sight. Knowing it was being handled and that I didn't have to face it alone nearly brought me to tears, and I said, "I was terrified of my past coming back around and hurting Romy. I didn't know how to keep him safe, but now...fuck, Adriano, that's just really amazing. Thank you, sincerely."

The fact that I was getting emotional definitely made him uncomfortable. "Don't mention it," he muttered. "Look, I'm going to go get Romy. Don't get all worked up." With that, he turned and fled.

A few seconds later, Romy returned. "I'm so proud of you," he said, as he caressed my cheek. "I was listening in, because I didn't know if I'd have to run in here and break up a fight. But you did great! You totally left your ego out of it, and you didn't get defensive."

"I surprised myself. The old me would have handled that very differently."

"It just goes to show how far you've come." He was right, and I felt really good about that.

Later that night, Romy carefully stretched out beside me on the bed and took my hand. After a while, he said, "I've been giving a lot of thought to what's next for us. What do you think about staying in San Francisco long-term?"

"I'm all for it, but won't you miss Las Vegas?"

"There are some things I'll definitely miss, like my friends, and having my mom close by. But after twenty-seven years in one place, I'm ready for a change."

As I stroked the back of his hand with my thumb, I said, "So, should we...I mean, did you want to..."

"Are you trying to ask if we'll live together?" When I nodded, Romy smiled at me. "That's a given. I need you with me, always."

He said those words so easily, but they were utterly life-altering. All my life, I'd traveled such a dark and lonely path. Now it felt like rounding a bend and seeing a bright new road opening up ahead of me. I knew there'd still be obstacles along the way. But I wouldn't be traveling it alone, and that made all the difference.

Epilogue: Romy

Six Months Later

"It's beautiful," Pete told me, as I panned my phone around the newly decorated living room in the home Marcus and I had just bought. "I love the blue-on-blue color scheme. It's very soothing."

"Thanks. There's still the entire second floor to tackle, but we feel great about the way it's all been coming together."

As soon as Marcus was well enough, we'd started house hunting. It ended up taking a few months to find the right place. But as soon as this gorgeous craftsman-style gem came on the market, we both knew we'd found our home.

I took a seat on the couch, and Pete grinned at me from my screen and said, "It's amazing, isn't it? You're a homeowner, I'm about to become a business owner, and we're both in love with hot, hunky men. Who'd have guessed we'd wind up here?"

"It's pretty wild."

Pete's expression grew serious, and he asked, "Are you sure you're okay with me buying your mom's bar? I know you said you were, but I also know what this place meant to you and your family."

"It definitely threw me for a loop when Mom said she wanted to sell it and retire," I admitted. "But I'm thrilled that she and her new husband are planning to travel, and that she's finally taking time for herself. And of course, I'm doubly thrilled she's selling it to you. It means she's keeping it in the family, and I know you and Guillermo are going to give it all the love it deserves."

"Aw, thanks for calling me family."

"It's what you are."

We chatted for a few more minutes, before Pete said, "I'd better go. My boyfriend's waiting on me to start a movie. I'll talk to you soon, and I'm looking forward to seeing you and Marcus when you come for a visit next month." It had taken a while for Pete to come around and believe Marcus could be trusted. Actually, that was true for everyone I knew. But he'd finally gotten there, and that made me happy.

After we said goodbye and ended the call, I went in search of my boyfriend and found him hard at work in the kitchen. "What's all this?" I asked, as I gestured at the numerous appetizers and snacks on the granite counter.

"Just a few munchies for poker night."

I came up behind him, and he turned to me and drew me into his arms as I asked, "Are you nervous about tonight?"

"A little. Since it's our first time entertaining—and because it's Adriano and Dante and their partners—I want everything to be perfect."

"It will be, and this all looks fantastic. That charcuterie board is a work of art."

He flashed me a smile. "I'm pretty sure you're teasing me, but it was fun to make."

"Nope, no teasing here. I love the way you've been discovering a passion for all things culinary, especially because I get to reap the benefits." I grinned at him as I swiped a piece of cheese from the tray.

The doorbell rang just then, and I raised a brow and said, "Someone's twenty minutes early."

"It's probably Adriano. He got the revised plans back from the architect, and he said he'd come over early to show me."

"In that case, you get the door, and I'll open the wine."

My brother and Marcus had ended up bonding over a pretty amazing project—an art center located in our old neighborhood, just a block from the bar. It turned out Art Giannopoulos was leaving his mark on Vegas after all, but in a way he'd never imagined.

The art center was going to include a permanent exhibit of the paintings and sculptures Art had collected over his lifetime—minus the pieces Marcus had already sold off. The funds he'd gotten from their sale had gone into purchasing an abandoned building, which was about to be rebuilt into an incredible resource for the community. In addition to providing studio space and a place for local artists to exhibit their work, it was going to offer free art classes for both kids and adults, taught by a staff of artists-in-residence.

There'd been a time when Adriano had been passionate about photography. His gorgeous photographs were still on display in the bar—and I was grateful that Pete had promised to keep them up when he bought the place. But aside from that, Adriano's love of photography had been all but forgotten, until Marcus came up with the idea for a community art center and asked for his help. That had prompted my brother to buy a new camera and start taking pictures again. I loved seeing him rediscover a part of himself that had been lost along the way.

When I finished opening several wine bottles, I returned to the living room and smiled at what I saw there. Adriano and Marcus were seated side-by-side on the sofa, gesturing at the blueprints strewn across the coffee table while carrying on an animated conversation. That project really had been the best thing for them, and the fact that they were bonding made me so happy.

Jack was perched on the arm of the sofa with a hand on his fiancé's shoulder, and he grinned at me and said, "Look, more blueprints." These were at least the sixth or seventh version.

Marcus looked up at me with excitement sparkling in his eyes.

"You have to see the new plans, baby! The architect took all of our notes, and she totally nailed it."

I squeezed in beside him, and Marcus and my brother explained the changes in great detail. They were like a couple of kids with a new toy, and their enthusiasm was infectious.

A few minutes later, I got up to answer a knock on the door. I expected Dante and Charlie, but what I found instead was Timothy, framed by two surfboards. "Look what I found today at a yard sale! One for me, one for you," he said. "I know they told us we wouldn't need our own boards for our beginner surfing lessons, but these were too cheap to pass up."

"Wow, thanks! They're really cool. Come on in." I carried one of the boards inside, while he brought the other.

After saying hello to everyone in the living room, Timothy turned to me and said, "Sorry, I should have called first. I didn't realize you had company."

"No, it's fine. Do you play poker? If so, you should join us."

Timothy lit up at the offer. "I'd love to."

My brother eyed the boards with a look of concern and asked me, "Does that mean you're going to go through with the surfing lessons?"

"Of course. Why wouldn't I?"

The frown line between his brows deepened. "Because the ocean is big, scary, and full of sharks, and you grew up in the desert. It's not like swimming in a pool, you know. Are you even comfortable around that much water?"

I grinned at him and said, "I'll be fine." Adriano had come a long way in terms of treating me like an adult, but he'd always be an overprotective big brother. That was just who he was.

Jack asked, "Does this mean you two have moved on from pole dancing?"

"No, we're still doing that twice a week," Timothy said. "Romy was just ready to add a new challenge, and this is what we came up with."

I'd signed up for a couple of classes through Open University, too. I still had no clue what I'd end up doing in terms of a career.

But while I figured it out, I'd been having fun learning new things, challenging myself, and continuing to build my confidence.

A few minutes later, Dante and Charlie arrived, and the poker game got underway. As usual, Adriano and Dante got way too into it, and the rest of us joked around and practically turned it into a drinking game.

At one point, Dante got a text and glanced at Marcus, and I asked, "Is everything alright?"

"Everything's spectacular," he assured me. "I'll tell you about it later." I assumed he didn't want to discuss whatever it was in front of Timothy.

Jack ended up beating all of us, by a lot. When the game ended, we started to relocate back to the living room, but Timothy told me, "I should get going. Mind if I leave the surfboards here for now?"

"That's totally fine. I'll bring them to our first class."

I walked him out to the front porch, and he gave me a hug and said, "Thanks for letting me be a part of your family poker night. That was a lot of fun."

"You're welcome to join us any time."

As he started down the stairs, he glanced at me over his shoulder and said, "The other reason I dropped by tonight was to tell you there's a smoking hot man who's been coming to the restaurant every night this week. He always makes a point of sitting in my section, and I really think he's into me, Romy."

"And you're just now telling me about him? I need details!"

"There aren't any yet. All I know is that he looks damn fine in his expensive suits. I'm willing to bet he looks damn fine out of them, too."

He grinned at me and waved goodbye as he started down the hill. I loved the fact that our home was walking distance to both the pink Victorian and the gorgeous Edwardian Adriano had recently bought for himself and Jack.

When I went back inside, Marcus smiled at me and said, "Good news. Dante's people finally tracked down Norton Gileki."

I took a seat on the arm of Marcus's chair and asked, "Where was he?"

Epilogue: Romy

"The slippery old fucker had run all the way to London." Dante looked very pleased with himself as he leaned back on the sofa and draped an arm around Charlie's shoulders. "He'd obviously already heard Marcus is under our family's protection, but I wanted to make sure he got the message in person, just so there's no misunderstanding."

"Impressive," I said, which made him puff up even more. "How'd you track him all the way to the UK?"

"It was easy. I'd had people monitoring his accounts, and he finally slipped up and used the wrong credit card—one that was under his real name," Dante explained. "I had a team of...let's just call them local, independent contractors rolling up on him less than two hours later."

"Is he still alive?"

Dante nodded. "All they did was put the fear of god into him. Apparently that resulted in a lot of sniveling, begging, and the possible soiling of some drawers. Gileki now very thoroughly understands he owes us a huge debt for letting him live."

He tried to keep his expression grave, as if all of this didn't absolutely delight him, but the sparkle in his dark eyes told a different story. It reminded me just how glad I was that he was on our side, because you did *not* want Dante Dombruso as an enemy.

"So, that's all of them," Marcus said. "You managed to track down every last one of Art's former associates. Romy's right, that's impressive."

Charlie was grinning as he got up and took his husband's hand. "You're sexy when you go all mob boss," he told him. "Let's go home and celebrate your victory."

Dante leapt to his feet. The heat between them was so intense that I almost expected them to start groping each other right then and there. "We're out of here. Thanks for hosting, Romy and Marcus. That's now your job forever, by the way, because those snacks were top notch." As they headed for the door, he called, "See you at Nana's for Sunday dinner. And Adriano, don't try to count tonight as a victory, just because your fiancé won. He's the poker prodigy, not you."

158

Adriano finished his glass of wine, and then he and Jack got to their feet. "We should go, too. Dante's right that you guys need to host every poker night from here on out, because you nailed it." As we walked them out, he told me, "Don't drown during your surfing lesson, and if you see a shark, punch it in the face."

That made me grin. "Great advice."

"I'm serious. I read that somewhere," Adriano said. "Marcus, I'll see you tomorrow for our video conference call with the architect."

My boyfriend nodded. "See you then."

On their way out the door, Adriano grinned and added, "By the way, I'm definitely claiming tonight as a victory over Dante. I may not have won, but since my brilliant fiancé did, I get partial credit."

Once they were gone, Marcus and I returned to the couch. I straddled his lap and kissed him before saying, "Well, clearly tonight was a total success. Thanks for going to all that effort."

"It was fun, and it meant a lot to me that everyone enjoyed it."

As I brushed his hair back from his eyes, I said, "That's really something about Dante's people tracking down Gileki all the way in England."

"It's a relief, now that Gileki's been found. I thought I'd let those concerns go when I first found out the Dombrusos would be backing me up. But I guess part of me was still holding my breath and waiting for the final pieces of that puzzle to fall into place. Now that they have, it feels like a weight's been lifted."

"Good. I'm glad you can finally let all of that go."

I ran my fingers into his hair and kissed him again. When we both started getting turned on, he asked, "Want to move this to the bedroom?"

"Uh, yeah!" He chuckled as I jumped off his lap and darted for the stairs.

In the middle of the night, after thoroughly wearing each other out, we curled up together under the covers. "I was thinking," I said, as

Marcus rubbed my back. "When we're in Vegas next month, want to pay a visit to the drive-through Elvis chapel?"

His face lit up with the most gorgeous smile. "Did you just ask me to marry you?"

"I did."

"The answer's yes, obviously."

"Woohoo!"

He laughed and kissed me, and we cuddled closer and started making plans. Instead of a formal reception, we decided to throw a big party after the ceremony with all our friends and family. Then we talked about all the romantic places we could go on our honeymoon.

After a while, Marcus grew serious and whispered, "It's hard to believe this is really my life."

"Why do you say that?"

"All those years when I was in prison, I lost hope. I stopped thinking about my future, and about the things I used to want so desperately, like finding love, being part of a family, or even just being happy. The simplest things, stuff most people would take for granted, felt so unrealistic that I let them go. I had to. Otherwise, the longing would have broken me.

"And now here I am, making plans with the man I love, who loves me in return. I feel like I'm living someone else's life, because mine can't be this wonderful."

I caressed his cheek and told him, "But this really is your life, and it's the one you deserved all along."

"Maybe I'll learn to believe that one day." He rested his forehead against mine and whispered, "But you'll never stop feeling like an absolute miracle."

The End

Made in the USA
Middletown, DE
30 April 2023

29781135R00096